T0129693

Decree of the Amulet

Margaret Gill

iUniverse, Inc.
Bloomington

DECREE OF THE AMULET

iUniverse books may be ordered through booksellers or by contacting:

iUniverse
1663 Liberty Drive
Bloomington, IN 47403
www.iuniverse.com
1-800-Authors (1-800-288-4677)

ISBN: 978-1-4759-4084-8 (sc)
ISBN: 978-1-4759-4085-5 (e)

Printed in the United States of America

iUniverse rev. date: 08/24/2012

Chapter 1

Davey woke abruptly, as the train came into Edinburgh. He stared out at the forbidding, grey, four storey houses either side of the track. They seemed the stuff of nightmares. He imagined himself locked away in one of those dark rooms trying to attract the attention of passengers on the train, yelling helplessly and hopelessly through barred windows knowing no one could hear him. By the time the train stopped he had convinced himself he was destined to be shut away, imprisoned, and starved into a premature death by his wicked uncle. He was in two minds to stay on the train. But no, he would face the enemy. He would insist on being sent back to his school, Brentwood, straight after the Easter holiday.

He got off the train reluctantly and gazed gloomily around, worrying about confronting his uncle when he felt, rather than saw, someone looking at him.

"Would you be David then?" a light Scots voice called.

He turned to see a slim young woman, with long hair the colour of corn, standing by the barrier. She was wearing a black woollen dress and a bright red shawl, which seemed to be covered in strange markings.

"I'm Mary, Mary McEwen," she said. "Your uncle's been delayed on business."

Davey took a deep breath. He was stunned by this attractive vision, at the same time tremendously relieved that his uncle had not come.

"Come on now, the car's waiting. I'm on short-term parking. We'd best haste young man."

Remembering the dream he'd had on the train, he hesitated for a brief second. But, he thought, there was no way she could ever be part of such a nightmare

Davey glanced at her. Mary McEwen was young and beautiful, not a bit like Uncle Eli who was old, mean, and crabby.

"You're wondering who I am, and why I should be sent to meet you?"

Davey nodded.

"Your uncle's secretary and general factotum. I look after all the accounts. Such a mess as you ever saw. But we'll soon sort that out; not your worry, mind. What you're worrying about is when you're going to get fed, eh?"

Davey blushed. He was getting very peckish. Tom, the school caretaker, who had taken Davey under his wing several years ago, after the plane crash that killed both his parents, had slipped him some sandwiches and some of Mrs Tom's famous chocolate cake, but that was ages ago.

"Let's get home first, if you can last out that long," she said leading the way to the parking lot.

"Wow! A Mercedes! Is this yours?"

"Mine? No way," she laughed. "Me? A poor working girl? No, this is one of your uncle's." As she ushered him towards the car he caught the fragrance of fresh woodland flowers.

"One? I thought he was … I mean, is, poor?" he stammered.

"Someone's been having you on my laddie. No, your uncle's stinking rich."

That didn't sound at all like the uncle he knew. Perhaps Mary had mistaken him for someone else. Perhaps she was meeting another David for another uncle

"Please stop," he said turning to her. "I think there's been some terrible mistake."

"A terrible mistake?" she began laughingly but broke off as she saw Davey's expression.

"Yes. I'm David Jampolski. My uncle is Eli Jampolski. You must have mistaken me for someone else."

"No mistake. It's David Jampolski I'm meeting for your Uncle Eli. Here's his note telling me which train to meet and he's signed it."

Davey immediately recognised the thin spidery handwriting, which had appeared every month with a note to say his pocket money was being reduced.

"We'll soon be back at the castle and then you'll be sure."

"Castle?" gulped Davey.

"Sure. Your uncle's a rich man, or," she added wryly, "he would be if we could get his accounts in order. But, as I said, that's my concern."

Davey climbed into the car and sank deeply into the luxuriously padded seat. But he still couldn't believe what he was hearing. Why had he been asked to leave school with his fees still unpaid? And why had he been summoned so curtly to Scotland without explanation? He knew only too well how mean his uncle could be. Why, he never even put the right amount of postage on his letters.

Soon Edinburgh was far behind. Davey must have dozed, for he woke with a start, as he became aware of the car slowing down and passing over a cattle grid.

"Well, we've made it! We're here," said Mary triumphantly.

Davey could just make out tall ferns on the sides of a long drive as the car twisted and turned upward. Through the darkness and drifting mist the hazy outline of turreted towers appeared, suddenly illuminated by a shaft of moonlight. This was really something, he thought, his tiredness disappearing in flash.

He remembered that the school caretaker, 'Uncle' Tom, so called by all the boys at school, had told him he was going to be visiting castles, and hunting in the forests. Had he known all along?

Mary heaved a sigh of relief. "Would you believe I hate driving?" she said as she opened the passenger door. Davey smelt the sweet scent of pine and heard the swish and ripple of a running stream. He took a deep breath and smiled. This was going to be terrific after all, especially with Mary around.

The next moment his hopes were dashed when she said, "Well here we are, Kilkune castle. I'll help you to the door and introduce you, then I must be off."

Davey swallowed his disappointment. Mary was so easy to be with. She made everything seem so much better. Having to leave Rob, his best friend, and his other pals had been an unpleasant shock. What on earth he wondered, was anyone as super as Mary doing as his uncle's secretary.

Mary knocked on the heavy metal studded door, which was opened by a sour looking woman dressed in a dull grey smock.

"Mr Jampolski's nephew, Davey," said Mary cheerily to the old woman using, as if she knew it, his mother's favourite pet name for him. "I think he's starving. Davey, meet Olga, your uncle's ....er...er... housekeeper."

He wanted to shout, "Don't go Mary, please stay," but, instead, he extended his hand politely, just grazing the long bony fingers of the old woman who did not make any comment except to nod and open the door a crack wider.

"Bye now Davey. I'll see you later."

The door clanged behind him and the light and brightness of Mary's presence went out like a snuffed candle flame. He could sense the whole weight of the castle on the top of his head pushing him down into oblivion. He felt alone in the dark pool of his shadow cast by the flickering flame from the lamp carried by the woman Olga. Suddenly he felt he was back in his nightmare on the train.

"You'll be in the turret room," said Olga, leading the way up winding stone stairs.

She spoke with a Polish accent reminding him of Dad. It was like a voice from the grave. It should have comforted him, but it only filled him with sadness and foreboding.

Dad had been a distant sort of parent and, because he was so much older, had not shared much with Davey. Davey had adored his mother Aya.

Aya was of French Polynesian extract, young, and full of fun. Davey's dark brown eyes that were so like Aya's, filled with tears as he remembered how she tossed her dark glossy hair and how her eyes danced when she laughed.

But the image of the past faded as fearful thoughts gripped him. He tried to concentrate on following the lamp as it bobbed ahead. Where was he being taken?

Olga, who was now at the top of the stairs stopped and pushed open a creaking door to reveal a sparse little room. The moon shone clear now through mullioned windows, revealing a wooden bed covered with a coarse blanket and a wooden chest of drawers. Davey's heart missed a beat as he recognised them both from his own bedroom in London. On the bedhead were painted figures of Polish dancers, a boy and a girl. The girl wore a garland of flowers and the same flowers appeared on the chest of drawers.

What were they doing here?

"You'll be wanting to eat," said Olga abruptly, interrupting his thoughts.

Davey nodded, numbed by the memories that were sweeping over him. He was wondering whether any of his old treasures were still inside the drawers when Olga thrust one his bags towards him with a grunt.

"There's a washbasin over in the corner," she said, holding the lamp so he could see. "When you're ready to come down take the corridor on the right at the bottom of the stairs. You'll come to a hall and the kitchen is straight ahead. Mrs McGraw will be there to find you something to eat."

She looked curiously at him for the second time since he'd arrived. Davey could feel her eyes searching him for some family resemblance, perhaps to his uncle. Under Olga's gaze he felt like an outcast, a hybrid. Perhaps he wasn't quite what she had been expecting. He knew he resembled his mother, Aya, with his dark skin, but he did have Karl's, his Polish father's, blonde hair. He was a sort of no man's land in himself, a mixture of nationalities, yet belonging to neither completely. He felt more like a displaced person here in this strange Scottish castle than he'd ever felt, nothing of him belonging anywhere, and no one who cared a fig about him.

"When will I be seeing my uncle?" he ventured anxiously. Uncle Eli, who Davey had only met once at his parents' funeral had given him the impression that he didn't like boys and as soon as he could had packed him off unceremoniously to Brentwood Boarding School.

"He'll be seeing you in the morning I expect," was her dour response.

"Am I to stay here?" asked Davey hoping that Olga might clarify how long he was to stay.

"Ay, this'll be your room for a while," she muttered misunderstanding him.

"Aren't there any light switches?" His voice showed surprise.

"You'll not be needing any light save the kerosene lamp. Your uncle doesn't hold with modern extravagances . . . . . . especially for boys."

"Why not for boys, ... Mrs Olga? . . . . . . I'm sorry I didn't catch your name."

"Didn't give it. No Mrs. . . .. Just Olga," she said, ignoring his question. "Remember, your uncle believes in economy. Strict economy."

Even in names, thought Davey wryly.

"Mind your step now. I'll leave the lamp. Don't want you having an accident on the stairs," she gave a hollow sort of laugh.

Left alone in the room Davey unpacked in the flickering light of the lamp. The room felt eerie and unfriendly with its stone walls and shadows. What had happened to all his parents' possessions? After the funeral he had been bundled off to Brentwood like a parcel. He'd once asked his uncle about their house in London and had received a short note to the effect that everything had been sold to meet his dad's debts. But why had he kept my bed and chest of drawers, Davey wondered. Had he always intended bringing me here? He had never been invited during school holidays. He'd stayed with his friend Rob or Uncle Tom, and sometimes he was invited to stay with other boys' parents, out of pity, he feared.

Davey opened the drawers one by one frantically searching for something, anything to call his own. He was disappointed to find nothing in the top drawer or the middle one, but right in the corner of the bottom drawer there was something. It was a small hard object, it was the turquoise amulet that his mother had always worn. It was such an immense treasure to find, something belonging to his past life. He folded his fingers round it tightly as though it was a magic talisman, the key to his lost past. Suddenly all the grief that had been pent up in him burst forth and, with tears welling, he lay down on the coarse blanket holding the amulet tightly.

Chapter 2

His rumbling insides soon reminded him that he had eaten nothing since the sandwiches on the train. Driven by hunger, Davey ventured down the stone steps, holding the lamp carefully. Turning right down a corridor, as Olga had instructed him, he came out into a vast hall where a table and chairs were shrouded in white sheets. He could just make out some animal heads on the walls and a few paintings and portraits. His lamp cast strange shadows and his footsteps echoed loudly as he crossed the hall. While he was deciding which of the doors leading off from the hall led to the kitchen, his eye was caught by a portrait of a young fair-haired boy dressed in national costume, like the Polish boy and girl dancers on his bedhead. Holding his lamp up close he thought the boy's eyes looked sad.

He supposed Olga's direction to go straight ahead must mean the middle door. Should he knock? He could hear no sound except the banging of his own heart against his ribs. Plucking up courage, he knocked loudly on the middle door. Since there was no reply he tried the door and found, to his surprise, that it opened up into a long room empty of chairs but having one vast table down the centre. Placing his lamp on the table Davey looked around, wondering what to do next, when he was startled by a hatch in the wall rattling open and a face poking through.

It was a friendly face belonging to a woman of middle age. There were daubs of flour on her nose and chin. She had thin sparse grey hair but her eyes twinkled.

"I'm Mrs McGraw and ye'll be Master Davey then," she said in a very broad Scots accent. "You're no like the master, though you've got the fair hair. I'd come round, but the kitchen door sticks. Could ye no shut yon door? It's my rheumatics. Can't abide draughts, and this castle is the mother of draughts, have ye no observed?"

Davey shook his head.

"I'll have something for ye to sup in no time, the kitchen fire's blazing. Ye'll be liking a wee drink o' tay? Set yeself down."

"But there's nowhere to sit," said Davey trying hard to understand all she said.

"Ay, ye can bring one of those chairs from the hall, laddie. Only the master and Olga eat in there. They keep all the rest covered up like a graveyard. By the time I get over there, what with me rheumatics and the blessed door, the food's gone cold. Olga grumbles, but he don't seem to notice what he eats. He's no a cheerful soul yer uncle."

She passed a bowl of steaming soup through the hatch.

"There's some tatties an some home made bread. Good old Scottish food, none of yer Polish stuff. *They* won't touch it," she said, indicating the food she had prepared for Davey.

"Everything is so quiet," he said glancing round nervously. "Aren't there any other servants?"

"Nay! Only me an Olga da Volga. But she's no servant, laddie, and don't ye forget it."

"Why do you call her Olga da Volga? Is that her real name?"

"Could be," she said enigmatically. "There's a lot here that could be. Could be better an' could be worse," she chuckled at her own little joke. "I knew if they brought ye here ye wouldna like it."

"I didn't say I didn't like it, Mrs McGraw," he said not wanting to upset her. "It's just different, and I miss my friends."

"Well there's me and my Billie and that Mary. Comes and goes as she pleases, but a right nice lassie. Ask her to take ye down to the village, find some lads of your own age. Then there's school."

"School… Mrs McGraw?"

"See, I'm rabbitting on and I don't ken what ye uncle has in mind for ye. I'm naught but an old chatterbox and ye mustn't mind me Davey. If ye've finished," she said looking at his empty plate, "I'd offer ye another helping, but the master says 'one helping's enough for anyone.' But seeing as ye're a big braw laddie, perhaps another wee helping won't go amiss,"she said ladling more soup into his bowl.

As she seemed inclined to go on talking, he asked about the portrait of the boy in the hall. "Is it my uncle as a boy?" Davey really hoped it was his own father, but Mrs McGraw just shut up suddenly like a clam.

"That's no yer uncle. Ye'll be hearing who that is along of a time," and she shut the hatch doors suddenly. There was a long silence. Davey was thinking he'd better just finish the soup and go back to his room when the hatch flew open again and Mrs McGraw's red face re-appeared.

"I've thought about it Davey, and it's best ye ken now. Yon portrait's of Boris, Uncle Eli's son."

"My cousin, Boris? Did he live here? Why is it best I know what now?" Not more mysteries, thought Davey.

"He didn't live here. Died in Poland, I believe. There's talk, only talk mind, that his death changed yer uncle's life. He doesn't like anyone to talk about Boris, so mind ye take care."

"If you hadn't told me I'd never have asked him."

"Just thought to guard ye. Don't be asking that Olga da Volga about him either. Remember, Mum's the word," and with that she shut the hatch again, loudly and firmly, making the lamp on the table quiver.

Davey made his way back to his room glancing uneasily at the animal heads, which cast strange shadows on the floor. He thought he saw grinning masks on the corridor walls. He stumbled back up the winding turret stairs feeling close to terror.

He spent a restless night, dreaming that he was being chased by disembodied stags' heads with evil red eyes. They chased him through thick pine forests and, to escape them, he pulled a red shawl around him embroidered all over with strange symbols, but it turned into a painting of a sad eyed boy with fair hair wearing Polish national costume. And still the stags came on; there was nowhere to hide.

Chapter 3

Davey awoke dry mouthed and blinking in the pale grey light of a Scottish morning. He felt imprisoned by the cold stone walls around him. If it had not been for the little diamond panes in the mullioned windows that shone and shimmered he would have felt as desolate as he had felt last night. Getting out of bed he found that if he looked out of his turreted window over the tops of the pines he could see the gleam of silver water. A loch, he thought, and at once he longed to explore but his heart fell as he remembered his uncle and he was again filled with dread. There was a knock at the door and Olga entered carrying a steaming jug.

"Here's your washing water. Hot water's precious here, don't waste it," she said, placing the jug next to his washstand.

Davey had never questioned the supply of water before. It came out of the tap regularly and plentifully, but Olga's pinched face indicated he'd better treat this water with respect.

"Breakfast is served in the Great Hall. Mind you're not late, 8.30 sharp," she said, turning her back on him and leaving without another word.

The Great Hall? That must be the hall with the paintings,

antlers, and stags' heads. He hurriedly washed and dressed. Would a T-shirt and trainers be appropriate for breakfast in the Great Hall? On second thoughts he pulled his grey school pullover on top of the T-shirt but left the trainers.

In the daylight Davey noticed the unevenness of the grey stone slab outside his door was not in line with the others. It was a wonder he'd managed not to trip in the dim light of the lamp last night.

He shivered as he entered the Great Hall and saw Olga sitting stiffly at the long table now darkly bare without the white covers of the previous night. She still had the grey smock on, but he was surprised to see she was wearing a pair of hooped gold earrings. Uncle Eli, a thin bent man, was standing in front of the stone fireplace reading a letter. He looked up as Davey crossed the hall; he folded and placed the letter in his pocket.

"David? You'll sit and eat with Olga and me. I've a deal to say to you, shortly. Don't heed Olga. I trust her with everything." The gold earrings clattered in approval. Davey did not know why but he shuddered involuntarily. His only clear memories of his uncle were from his mean stingy little notes to him at school suggesting he must be more careful how he spent his monthly allowance, and once he had actually enquired about his health, a query that had puzzled him. He was a good head taller than most of the boys in his year, played all sports energetically and well, ate well, slept well, and could think of no earthly reason why anyone should worry about his state of health. He recalled his rage at being removed from school before the year had ended and how humiliated he had felt at being told that the school had still received no payment of fees for the year.

Just then Mrs McGraw came in with a basket of bread. Davey noticed the bread was a very dark colour, almost black, and there was no butter on the table. He watched as Eli sliced the bread thinly and handed him a slice with a boiled egg. Both Eli and Olga ate the dark bread and eggs silently without looking at him.

"Take a drink then lad," said his uncle finally, pointing to the glass jug of water Mrs McGraw had just brought in. "Mrs McGraw's too fond of making what she calls a pot of tay. Wasteful and unnecessary for the health. And I take it you're in good health?"

"Oh, yes, Uncle," Davey said bridling.

"Tea is very wasteful." Uncle Eli pointed to the cook's disappearing form. "The world's full of wastrels spending money, going to la di dah schools and the like. Hard work, that's what's wanted. Too many layabouts cadging money from the country." He sniffed loudly as he helped himself to a glass of water. "In Poland the State gave you nothing, nothing. Then after the war the Communists came . . . took everything. Your granddad was a thrifty man. Transferred everything to the Swiss banks, just in time."

Davey could hear the bitterness in his uncle's voice. There was also something in his tone he didn't quite understand.

"But you wouldn't know about that would you, with your soft silly mother. Spoilt, that's what she was, and you too. No grit, no Polish grit in you."

Olga smirked.

How dare he insult his mother, thought Davey furiously. He knew Eli didn't want him here and didn't even pretend to like him. He hadn't asked to come in the first place. He tried hard to stifle a desire to thump his uncle, swallowing so hard it came out as a hiccup.

"Rich food, that's what's your trouble and the trouble of half the folks in this country," said Uncle Eli. "You'll not be getting that here. Good plain food, eh, Olga?"

Davey was very fond of food. He remembered tea with Uncle Tom and Rob at the school Lodge with a real pang. No doubt Brentwood was one of the lah di dah schools his uncle had referred to. It was hardly the right moment to ask if he was ever going back there.

"I've just had a letter from your teacher Mr.Bartlett," said Eli uncannily picking up on Davey's thoughts. "He says you play excellent rugger and that you will be missed for your good sportsmanship and friendliness. That's not the sort of report I expect from a school that charges more per term than I pay all the servants in this place for a year."

Davey looked round the hall, imagining all the servants shrinking back into their laundries, stables and store rooms, except that he knew there were no servants, only Mrs McGraw.

"Friendliness, sportsmanship! What do you call that? What about maths and accounting. Eh?"

"Not very good at those uncle," said Davey, angrily biting his lip.

"Money, that's what matters boy, getting your values right, having a good business head, understanding a bargain. Never one to miss a bargain is Olga."

Olga twisted her bony fingers and seemed almost to smile. Eli tapped his fingers on the middle of his forehead. "That's what the boy needs Olga. Some lessons in practical know-how."

Olga's smile was now a grimace and Davey saw her glance at the portrait of the fair-haired Polish boy. He wondered whether Boris had been good at maths.

"Mary McEwen," Davey looked up, so surprised to hear an unaccustomed gentleness creeping into his uncle's voice as he said the name. "A wizard, no, an angel ….. an accounting angel."

Davey glanced at Olga, at the same time noticing a hard glint of something that could have been jealousy in her eyes. She got up and left the table, her earrings clattering ominously.

"You'll be wondering why your old Polish uncle could be asking you up here," said Eli with a sly look.

Still not the right time to ask about Brentwood, thought Davey looking straight into his uncle's hard grey eyes and finding Uncle Eli avoided looking directly at him. Davey just nodded and waited.

"We have things to talk about David, lawyer's things. Get Mary to come and give you some details, eh? That girl's got sense, understands things, a good business head." He repeated this to himself several times as if savouring it. "We'll be away a few days, Olga and me. Business, you know. Mrs McGraw'll see to the food. Olga will arrange that. Can't have riot in the larder while we're away. She's a wastrel that woman McGraw .....a wastrel. Can't have you wasting your time either."

"But, Uncle, it's the holidays." Davey was already planning to go exploring and perhaps even go down to the loch he'd seen in the distance.

"Holidays! Nonsense boy. Keep busy, keep your nose to the grindstone. Earn your keep. Holidays indeed. Make yourself useful, keep out of mischief. There's wood to be stacked. Billy McGraw comes in to cut the pines, but he needs help sorting and stacking."

Davey glowered at his uncle. He was feeling sullen and angry. He'd been so looking forward to having some free time to wander through the pine forest.

As though he had again read his mind Eli said, "And don't go off getting lost or down to the loch. There's some dangerous swamp and you could be up to your neck before you know it."

Davey couldn't be sure whether his uncle was trying to warn him or challenge him. Perhaps he even wanted him to get lost as he didn't seem to approve of anything about him.

Eli rang a brass bell on the dining table and Mrs McGraw shuffled in with a tray. "Get Billy to show David how to help with

the logs. And no wasting things or any tittle tattle while we're away."
Eli, leaning heavily on his stick, made his way across the hall without
saying anything about the important matters he'd been going to talk
to Davey about.

"Fat chance to waste anything," said Mrs McGraw, not caring
whether Eli was still in earshot or not. "I'd have left years ago if I'd
had any sense. Don't fret laddie, I'll no be serving you that foreign
muck while's they're away," and she grinned.

Davey smiled back. They were both going to enjoy their
freedom.

Back in his little tower room Davey tore a page out of one of
his old school notebooks and began to write to his best friend Rob.
If only his uncle had allowed him to have a mobile like his friends.
It was really weird his uncle living without any connection with the
modern world, but if Mary had an office she must have a computer.
He'd ask her if he could email Rob, but in the meantime he'd get his
thoughts down on paper.

'Hi Rob,

Hope things are going well. Scotland could be worse, I suppose.
Can you believe my uncle actually lives in a castle? Thinks he can keep
me cooped up here. Soon as I get the chance I'm off exploring.

Met an amazing person called Mary. She can charm the birds off
the trees, even has Uncle eating out of her hand. She says Uncle's really
rich. Can you believe that? Then there's Olga, the housekeeper, who
doesn't go overboard on me, but the cook's fun and jolly. She has a son
Billy who does the rough work but he doesn't sound terribly bright,
so I don't thnk he'll be much company. Oh! and I've got a room in a
tower looking over the pine forest. And there's some sort of mystery
about my cousin Boris. When I asked about his portrait, it caused
quite a stir. Wonder why?

Haven't asked about coming back to school yet, but I'm not giving up.

Say hello to Uncle Tom and Mrs. Tom.

P.S. Uncle Eli's going to be away for a few days, so while "the cat's away….etc."

Get in touch soon. I'm sure Mary will let me use her lap top. Sorry there's no phone.'

On second thoughts he scribbled out the references to Mary.

Just then he heard the sound of a car and, bounding to the window, glimpsed his uncle in a black limousine, surely the Mercedes, driving up to the main door. He got out and stood tapping the bonnet impatiently. Then he strode across the drive to the main entrance. Davey, hearing a loud clang, cautiously opened his door and heard Eli speaking in a tone of voice that suggested he was at the end of his patience.

"What on earth are you dithering about woman?"

"Won't be a moment." It was Olga. "I'm just coming."

"You know Stefan's warned us the environmental agency's already on to us. We can't get the wrong side of the board of directors by turning up late."

"That's their responsibility Eli, they're just using you."

"Come on now, must get going, can't take the risk. The fines would be enormous. It would ruin us...ruin us."

The door slammed and Davey watched as his uncle and Olga drove off through the trees.

Wonder what that was all about he thought closing his door. Hadn't Mary said Uncle Eli was rich, yet it seemed some fines would ruin him? And who was Stefan?

There were three windows in the little round tower room. Through the West window he could see the topmost branches of a huge cedar tree which touched the window ledge making eerie grating sounds. Beyond, the grounds sloped down to the dark pinewoods and, for a moment, Davey was startled as he thought he saw someone moving there, but then he realised there was no one. The pine trees looked tightly packed, dark and threatening like some vast monster waiting to attack. A thin column of smoke was eddying up and twisting and writhing like a snake. In the far distance the sun was picking out the silvery gleam of the loch. His pulse quickened.

Returning to the window overlooking the drive to ensure that his uncle really had gone he saw Mary approaching and he rushed down to meet her.

"Well Davey. How goes it?" She was wearing an old grey sweater and jeans, but there was nothing ordinary about Mary. When she looked at him he had the feeling she seemed to know everything about him. There was a gravity in her manner and such a profound quietness about her, it unnerved him.

"What have you got planned for today?" she asked.

"I'd like to go exploring, but I've been left work to do, haven't I?"

"I have your uncle's instructions." She laughed, "but you deserve to have some free time to settle yourself in. Come into the hall. I have a plan of the castle and the surrounding area and can tell you all you need to know."

She rang the little bell on the huge dining table and Mrs McGraw came in with steaming cups of frothy coffee, fresh pancakes and a bowl of honey and brown sugar.

"A little spoiling for the laddie," she grinned. "Ye'll no get much o' that here. But while Mary's in charge anything's possible."

And indeed Davey was beginning to think that was true. Davey noticed that while he was enjoying the pancakes and honey, Mary ate nothing. She toyed with her coffee but didn't drink it. He was aware, in the daylight, how fine and transparent her skin was. There was a strange glow of light about her and there, again, was that fresh woodland smell.

Davey finished off the pile of pancakes while Mary plied him with questions about school and his friends.

"It would be great to speak to my best friend, Rob," he said, "but there's no phone."

"Hm!" said Mary thoughtfully. "You find that odd?"

"Among other things, like no electricity, hot water, servants, yet a castle and posh cars, and," he added shyly, "yourself."

"You find me odd?" she laughed.

"No," he stammered blushing. "You're not odd........but you don't, sort of, fit in."

"Hm!" she said again, gazing at him intently with her fine green eyes. "Nothing is as you expected?"

"Some things. Uncle Eli hasn't changed for a start, but there's Olga... she's weird. And then there's Boris."

"Boris? Take a look at his portrait over there and tell me exactly what you see. Go on," she urged as Davey hesitated.

Davey got up from the table feeling strangely uneasy at this request. He hadn't really studied the painting in daylight.

"Well?" queried Mary, watching him closely as he looked up at the painting.

"I see a boy, much younger than me, about eleven, twelve, maybe younger. He's got blond hair and he's wearing national costume."

"Yes?" said Mary.

Davey saw now. It was a full-length portrait and Boris was clearly a cripple. Both his legs were in irons and the stick Davey had thought was part of the dancer's outfit, was obviously a walking stick.

"Boris was born with a deformity, the result of an explosion, caused by an experiment into a revolutionary new type of fuel. He died shortly after this portrait was painted." Davey saw something akin to pity in Mary's eyes as she spoke. "Eli loved the boy deeply. Such loss can do strange things to people. Don't forget that."

Did that explain the tension between him and Eli, the rage and grief running under it all? He felt almost ashamed of having such a hatred of his uncle.

Then as she gazed at him he realised that she was also speaking about his own loss. Her eyes were moist and tender as she enfolded him for a moment in her arms like a mother.

"And now for the castle," she said in a brisker tone and disengaging herself gently. "It's probably no more than two hundred years old. Not old, as castles go."

She spread a sketch out on the long dining table. Indeed, it didn't look like a castle at all, more like a manor house, except that it had two turreted towers. The central hall was sandwiched between the towers and had steps that led down to the main door which opened up on to a gravel drive and lawns that swept down to the pinewoods he had glimpsed from his room. The peculiarity of the main hall was the gallery that followed the entire upper part of the hall and led off into various rooms.

"Is there an office in the castle where you work?"

"A small room of sorts, yes," she replied.

"I was hoping, maybe, I could send my friend Rob an email."

"Of course. That could be arranged. No problem."

"This," she said, pointing to the second tower, "is Eli and Olga's room."

Davey gasped audibly. "Olga, the housekeeper?"

"It's all right Davey, they're man and wife. They were not legally married until some few years ago. Your uncle still has a tendency to treat Olga like the servant she once was. Now is there anything else you want to know about?"

22

"The woods, the loch ....everything."

"Everything? That could take some time," she said laughing as she folded up the sketch.

Together she and Davey walked down the steps, through the main door, and out onto the sloping lawns.

"Where would you like to begin?"

"The loch, please, Mary."

"In that case I'll just go and warn Mrs McGraw that we won't be back in time for dinner."

Chapter 4

They took a path that wound down through a broken gate and, pushing their way through mounds of bracken, came onto a wooded slope.

"It's rough going underfoot from now on. Good thing you're wearing trainers, though boots would have been better," said Mary.

Davey saw that there was no clearly defined path ahead, but Mary nimbly picked her way through the trees. Often open patches of flinty stone gave the appearance of a path but Mary ignored all side tracks and forged straight on, leading on and on into the depths of a wood that got deeper and darker as they journeyed on, until only small glimpses of sky could be seen.

Although Davey was very fit he was soon panting with the exertion of pushing through dense undergrowth.

It seemed ages before they came to the edge of a clearing on the hillside where suddenly there was a steep pit or quarry strewn with rocks and boulders. An unwary wanderer through these woods could be in for a nasty shock, thought Davey.

"Unsightly and cruel," Mary shuddered.

Unsightly, Davey agreed, but cruel seemed a strange word.

"Tearing up the earth, destroying the natural habitat of wild life." Mary's voice sounded so harsh and angry that he looked at her in surprise and saw that her eyes had tears in them. And around her he thought he detected a smell like the stifling smell of burning crops. She looked so different now like a frightened young deer. He was aware also that on the entire journey she had not been out of breath for a single moment.

"Mary?" he began, and then faltered, not wanting to ask the question that had risen almost unbidden.

"Your uncle? Is that what you want to know?" Her voice, usually so light and happy, trembled. "Yes, this is your uncle's doing. You'll find more of these terrible wounds scarring the landscape. This is dangerous territory for a stranger. But come on," she said, regaining her composure. "If we're to make the loch before the afternoon we'd better press on."

Now they were climbing over rocks and pushing their way through thick brambles, but the light had returned. They were out of the deepest part of the wood and ahead Davey could make out the gleaming silver water of the loch.

"Watch out for marsh and swampy areas. There's some filthy dangerous bog around here," said Mary, as they tramped through thick grasses and reeds. "They call it Deadman's Bog."

"Hey!" Davey called in alarm as the grass ahead flattened and long coils of green shot towards them. "Mary, look out!" He yelled, horrified to see a darting writhing mass surrounding her.

"Grass snakes, no need for alarm."

To his astonishment, while Mary's eyes seemed to darken, she appeared to be smiling. He watched fascinated. The snakes coiled up around her as she stroked them tenderly. Then slithered away, disappearing as suddenly as they had come.

"Whew!" Davey whistled under his breath. "You weren't afraid at all. You even touched them."

Mary only smiled a deep, secret smile as they picked their way past the marsh to a tiny sandy bay where the loch waters lapped gently.

"An apple, fruit cake and Coke," said Mary, producing them from the small haversack she carried. "A present from Mrs McGraw. Said she couldn't let you starve when I went to tell her we wouldn't make dinner."

"My uncle called you a wizard. He's right," said Davey, tucking into the cake. It tasted just like Mrs Tom used to make, and memories of Wednesday half days at the School Lodge with Rob and Uncle Tom filled him with nostalgia.

The sun was gleaming fitfully, occasionally pushing its rays through the clouds. Now and again a strong shaft of sunlight penetrated burning through the grey clouds, sharpening the reflections of trees and bushes in the water. Davey became aware of the strange fact that while his own elongated shadow appeared on the water Mary's did not. But when he pointed this out, Mary simply shrugged her shoulders and said, "I expect it's just a trick of the light."

He was about to counter with proving the impossibility of this when he heard someone hailing them from the opposite bank.

Mary stood up shielding her eyes, trying to pick out who it was.

"He's pointing to the direction we've come in," said Davey. "What's he trying to say?"

"It's the marsh. It looks much blacker than when we came through and the blackness seems to be spreading. It looks as if it's spreading over the track we came on. It seems to be seeping further and further at quite a rate. Quick let's go." Mary grabbed the haversack and Davey rushed after her towards the seething marshy water now blocking their way completely.

"To go all the way round the loch will take hours. But we have no option. Best foot forward from now on Davey."

The figure who had been waving to them was coming rapidly round the end of the loch towards them.

"Why, it's the laird himself," exclaimed Mary.

An old man, with long grey hair and a short stubbly beard, clad in tartan kilt and thick navy coloured jersey was approaching with long youthful strides despite his venerable appearance.

As he came nearer Davey was surprised to realise he recognised the old man's face. Where had he seen him before?

"Ye'll no be going back that way lassie. Thought to warn ye. There's been some odd goings on yon side of the loch. Something's eating up the banks of the loch at an alarming rate. Soon yon bank'll be all bog. Sometimes, like today, when we get a wee bit of sun it seems to get worse. No one seems to know what's going on. Can't be pollution, there's no industry around for miles. Wish to God I knew what or who was behind it. If it doesn't clear soon the fishing'll be quite spoilt." He lashed out angrily at the reeds with the knobbed stick he was carrying. "Are ye from afar? But now I think on it, I reckon I've seen your bonny face in Lochlan."

"Kilkune," Mary corrected him.

"That's quite a step for ye both. The Landrover's nigh at hand. Will ye no accept a lift from an auld neighbour?"

"From the Laird of Lochlan? We'd be honoured," said Mary.

As Davey paced beside the two of them who were both striding out at quite a rate, Mary with her lithe, loping movements and the Laird with a firm strong athletic swing, he puzzled again over the familiarity of the old man's face.

When they came to the pull-in where the Landrover was parked something the laird said jogged his memory.

"The laddie's no a Scot. Must be a Sassenach up for the holidays, ay lad?

That was it, the word Sassenach. Now Davey remembered. At the last Speech Day the man presenting the prizes had used that very word. Of course, it had been him, he remembered now, it had been the Laird of Lochlan.

"On holiday from Brentwood School," he said.

"Brentwood, Cheshire? Fine school, fine headmaster Mr Hughes. Who was your housemaster?"

"Mr Bartlett."

"Remember him well. Give him my regards when ye get back."

"I don't think I'm going back."

"Not going back? Why ever not? Ye're a slacker? Been suspended, eh?"

"Nothing like that sir,"

"You'll have to speak to Mr Jampolski," broke in Mary, noting Davey's embarrassment, "Davey's uncle."

He noticed when Mary mentioned his uncle's name she and the Laird exchanged knowing glances.

"And that I'll do," he said, revving up the engine and speeding off round the loch at breakneck speed. Soon they were hurtling up the hillside and through the pines, Davey grasped the handgrip tightly as the wheels hit the uneven road, seeming to follow a flight path rather than the road.

Mrs McGraw, who must have heard the squeal of brakes as the Landrover came to a halt, came rushing out onto the gravel drive. "I'd just started to worrit," she began, breaking off when she saw the laird helping Mary down from the front passenger seat. "Oh, the Laird himself. Come right in an I'll soon have a pot o' tay ready." She bustled away, not waiting for an answer. But the Laird called after her that he'd no be stopping today.

"The old rogue," said Mrs McGraw when they were all sitting sipping tea. "They say he canna be trusted with the lassies despite his age. He's got a reputation for living in the fast lane. Ye maun take care Mary."

"I can take care of myself, thank you Mrs McGraw," replied Mary acidly.

But Davey guessed Mrs McGraw wasn't sensitive to tone of voice. She'd lived at Kilkune castle too long to be wounded by a harsh retort. Nevertheless, she left them to themselves as she cleared the table and returned to the kitchen.

Davey tried to ask Mary about the quarry and to get her to comment on the black marsh, but her mouth was set in a hard firm line. She said she didn't want to talk now, she was tired.

Davey had the feeling that her moods and expressions were as changeable as the waters of the loch itself. He seemed not to know her. This was not the Mary who had set out with him that morning. He was almost afraid of her deep mysteriousness and her way of not answering directly. He still didn't believe her 'trick of the light' comment. He was aware that there was a cold grey frightening side to her.

Chapter 5

Davey had overslept. He was wakened by a loud screech of brakes on the gravel. Could it be his uncle back already? He rubbed his eyes. His head hurt and he felt out of sorts. Looking out of the window facing onto the drive he saw a strange lorry had drawn up. A rough looking man in a singlet, with tattoos all over his arms, was jumping out of the driver's cab. Then Davey saw Mrs McGraw. Unfortunately he was too far away to hear what was being said but the man looked very angry and was making wild gestures. After a few minutes he heard someone coming up the stairs and opened his door to see Mrs McGraw, extremely red in the face and panting as she climbed up the steps. "Can ye come down, laddie. My Billie's worrit... It's a matter of urgency."

"I'm not dressed, but I'll be with you straight away." Davey hastily threw his anorak over his pyjamas.

Just as Davey reached the drive, he saw a stocky thick set youth whom he assumed was Billy McGraw approaching with a puzzled expression on his face. "What the b...blazes is that lorry doing here?" said Billy, ignoring Davey. His mother was clucking like a flustered hen and the driver, arms akimbo, was staring at them both belligerently.

Davey noted how like his mother Billy was, with his round open face and how slow and laboured his speech was.

"There shouldna' be a d…delivery while master's awa," said Billy looking the driver straight in the eye.

"An I canna help that," came the reply. "Instructions were to deliver, and I'll be needing a signature. A lorry were sent last night and had to turn back, as no one bothered to answer the door, but I'm no going back without a signature."

"Well, here's the master's nephew wi' the same surname," said Mrs McGraw, edgily," he's been left in charge so he'll have to sign."

"It'll do," said the driver, producing a chit of paper from his trouser pocket.

"Come Master David. Ye'll hae to sign here." Mrs McGraw was looking decidedly nervous as she took the pen from the driver and handed it to Davey.

"What am I signing for?" he asked glancing at the heading, Imperial Fuel Company.

"Best ask no questions laddie but do it anyway," she urged him.

Davey, seeing only confusion in her face but trusting in her honesty, signed D. Jampolski and the driver, satisfied, trundled up the back hatch of his lorry, while Billy helped to unload dozens of shiny unlabelled metal containers onto the drive. Davey was surprised to see how carefully the rough looking man handled the containers as if they were crates of eggs.

"Breakfast lads," said Mrs McGraw, as soon as the lorry had been driven away. "When Master David's ready."

"I'm ready now," he said, "but I'd like to get dressed. I'll not be a minute."

Sitting in the long hall with Billy and his mother, eating porridge with honey and cream and freshly baked bread, Davey felt his ill humour of the morning disappearing fast.

"The auld cattle man brings me fresh cream, flour and oats if I bake him fresh bread in exchange. Enjoy it while ye can."

"Who makes the black bread?" asked Davey.

"Not me. There's a shop in Dunkeld gets it special from a continental bakery in Edinburgh. Mary picks it up for yer uncle."

"Does she live in Dunkeld?"

"She could an she could na'. It's a mystery where she goes to."

Billy looked at Davey as though he was thinking hard.

"Could d…do wi' some help loading," was all he said.

He lumbered off in the direction of the long sheds that Davey thought must serve as garages.

"My Billy's good wi his hands but not like ye, he's had no schooling. Doesn't take it all in easy. But go on laddie. He'll be pleased for yer help."

Sure enough, when Davey arrived outside Billy had pushed up one of the overhead doors and soon Davey heard what he thought was a tractor starting up. There was a truck coupled to the tractor and Billy, jumping out of the driver's cab began, with Davey's help, to carefully load the metal containers into the truck.

"What's inside?" asked Davey.

"D dunno, but we have to be careful not to tip 'em Mr Eli said. Hop in!" said Billy when they were all loaded. "We'll leave them d… down by the quarry."

"The quarry? I was there yesterday with Mary. You can't get down there with a tractor."

"There's a…a proper track runs right round the woods right down to the quarry. Hop in, ye'll see."

Billy started up the tractor and soon they were heading out towards the eastern side of the estate. The gravel drive gave way to a wide tarmac road that curved eastwards and skirted right round the pinewoods.

"Whoa!" said Billy, braking suddenly as the quarry came in view.

Davey noticed a pulley and a gantry and some sort of a loading bay at the edge of the quarry that he hadn't seen before, but Mary had said there were other quarries so perhaps this wasn't the same one he had seen.

"Some men from Lochlan come over to do the loading." Billy said stuttering. "All I do is o... off-load these for them. Give us a hand a... and b... be careful, mind!"

Billy passed the containers down from the truck and David stacked them. Davey's hands were getting hot and sticky and he was finding it more and more difficult to hang on to the shiny metal. Then suddenly he was caught unawares as a slippery container slid out of his grasp. He watched horrified as it bounced down the steep quarry side. There was a sickening thud as it hit the bottom, a violent explosive sound as shale, small rocks and clouds of choking sickening fumes enveloped them.

"Bleedin' 'ell!" yelled Billy as they ran coughing and spluttering into the woods behind them. "I'll b...be in for a right 'earful when yer uncle gets b...back."

Davey knew that whatever was in the metal tins was none of his business, but he felt uneasy. He remembered his uncle's words about industrial waste while trying hard to dismiss the idea that there was anything wrong with them. There were enough mysteries without imagining any more.

"It mightn't be noticed," he said hopefully once they were clear of the billowing smoke and fumes.

"Oh! It'll be... noticed all right. All these are checked and double checked by the... Lochlan men."

"What do they do with them when they've checked them?"

"S...s...search me laddie. I only ken what I have to do. I d... don't ask questions."

Davey was aware of an odd sensation like a shiver down his spine. He turned nervously looking into the depths of the pine forest. This was not the first time during his stay in Kilkune that he'd had this sensation of being watched. He stared into the darkness but could see no movement.

"Are there animals in this part of the forest?" he asked.

"Nothing d...d... dangerous, a few rabbits, and grouse in season, why?"

"I thought something was watching us. I thought I saw something."

"What do you m...mean, watching us? Could be the B...B...Broch Barach," said Billy in a quavery voice.

"What's that?"

"They say how it comes out of the loch at times. It's like a huge s...s... serpent an' it crawls 'long looking for victims. There are stories about B...Broch turning into a horse and letting children ride upon his back, then d...d...diving into the loch an' diving deep down wi 'em."

"Of course, you're joking," said Davey, feeling less frightened by this superstitious legend than he had been a few moments ago.

"Nay, but it's true. Their l...l...livers was found floating on the surface. Folk round here believe in the loch monster and in many other things I could show ye. Come on, I'll show ye." Billy took hold of Davey's arm and began leading him towards the forest. "There are the s...s...sacred places fer instance. Would ye like to see one?"

"What about your tractor?" Davey wasn't too keen to discover Billy's sacred places.

"It'll be fine till we return. Come on then."

Soon they came to a clearing in the forest. The tattered remains of pines and oaks around the open space looked as though they had been there undisturbed for centuries.

"'Tis the wild wood itself," whispered Billy in awe. "Ye must keep hush an'cross yeself in the w...wild wood if ye want to be s....s.... safe."

Davey was no stranger to making the sign of the cross but he was surprised at Billy's need to do so. He did as he was told, then caught his breath in astonishment as they came to an overgrown patch at the edge of the clearing where two monstrous boulders, covered in moss and lichen, seemed to rise up mysteriously before them. Pulling the thick brambles and overgrown grasses away, Billy revealed a round moss-covered hole in the ground.

"It's a holy well. Folk come here to be cured of their ailments, rheumatics, and the like. There's a store o' magic in these places, especially, folk say, in them ancient trees. Old Alistair who lives in the village is a d...d...diviner, an' he's always coming across magic places. Now do ye ken what that is?" he said pointing to a small cup-like boulder.

But Davey wasn't listening. He was suddenly riveted by the appearance of a faint symbol on one of the larger boulders. It was like a man's face with snakes or leaves or twigs radiating out from his brow and around his entire face. "Acholiwai," he muttered.

"What?"

"The Acholiwai, symbol of the god of the trees and the plants. There, on that boulder."

"That isn't what they call it round here."

"But I can show you," Davey fumbled excitedly in his back pocket drawing out a little folded pouch and showing Billy the treasured photo of Aya which he always carried with him. See round her neck she is wearing the Acholiwai amulet. I have it in my room. I'll show you."

The amulet was too indistinct to make out, but Billy was clearly struck by the amazing beauty of Aya's face. "Who's that then?"

"My mother," said Davey, "aware that Billy was looking first at the photo, at Aya's dark features, skin and hair and then at Davey.

Billy whistled under his breath "She's no a Sassenach."

"She came from the Polynesian islands where they had many magical things like Acholiwai, all sorts of healers and firewalkers and........." Davey broke off. Billy was staring at him with a petrified sort of look.

From the darkest part of the forest came a strange rustling and pattering noise. Billy's eyes were wide and staring with fright.

"It's nothing," said Davey, "just leaves and things blowing in the wind."

"S...sh! Be quiet! J...j...just listen."

"I can't hear anything now."

"S...s...something moving ...out there in the wood."

The thudding in Davey's heart drowned all sound.

A twig cracked.

Billy gripped Davey's hand.

"It's just deer... that's all," said Davey.

Billy's face had gone white. "Nah! It's the B...B...Broch...it's coming for us." He stumbled to his feet scrambling though bracken and stumbling over stones in his haste to get away.

Davey, with heart still throbbing wildly but refusing to show a coward's heels, stood his ground. It was bound to be some wild creature they'd disturbed. He wasn't going to allow himself to be persuaded by Billy's superstitious tale of the Broch. Pushing past the tangled undergrowth surrounding the stone he peered through the leaves.

It was too dim and shadowy to make anything out, but then he heard a loud rustling and picked out something moving. There were several dark shapes in the distance, surely they were not animals. A sudden shaft of bright sunlight shone through the trees and he realised with a gasp of relief that they were human figures. Perhaps they were quarry men who had been alerted by the explosion.

He found Billy seated in the tractor, gripping the steering so hard his knuckles showed white. Thin wisps of smoke and fumes were still eddying from the quarry.

"I told you it was nothing, just a group of quarry men," Davey said climbing up beside him.

"No...no... there weren't anyone on d...d...duty today. There shouldna' have been anyone. I tell ye it was the shadow of the m...m... monster."

Since there was no point in arguing with him they drove back to the castle in silence except for repeated outbursts from Billy with his "I swear it was the B...B...Broch." Davey kept his counsel. His mind was far too busy going over the events of the day and he was both puzzled and worried. What could his uncle be up to? If only he could phone Rob or Tom. He needed to speak to someone. Perhaps he would ask Mary about it when she came next time.

"Look ye," said Billy when they arrived back at the garage. "We've not started on the logs yet. There's a lot of work to do. But I'll go get my saw 'cos there's a patch o' trees I need to cut first."

While Billy went to fetch his tools Davey went to his room. He wanted to have a look at his mother's amulet again to compare it with what he'd seen on the standing stone. He noticed the bottom drawer was slightly ajar. He really ought to be more careful, it was such a precious thing. He took the amulet out and studied it carefully. What a strange coincidence that the engraved face of the

Polynesian god should resemble that of one carved on a remote Scottish boulder. Then, with extra special care, he brought his holdall out from under the bed and, unzipping an inside pocket, placed the amulet inside and zipped it up again securing the tag with a safety lock.

Chapter 6

Eli and Olga Jampolski landed by helicopter on the private island of Torksay off the far tip of the West coast of Scotland. They had been delayed several days on the mainland at the depot sorting out paperwork regarding deliveries of waste to be disposed of in the Highlands. They were met on the tiny tarmac strip by a fussy, sandy haired man who, trying to assist Eli, kept getting in the way of his walking stick. "Damn fool," muttered Eli audibly.

Eli was not looking forward to this meeting of the directors of the Imperial Fuel Company. He knew they were keeping something from him. Irritated beyond measure by the delay at the depot he was not going to stand any nonsense from the board of directors. They would have to take responsibility. He wasn't going to. He was already in deep financial trouble. He knew from information leaked by Olga's cousin, a scientist employed by the company, that the Scottish Environmental Agency was onto him. This could only mean that his income, already dwindling, would be severely cut if they caught up with him. The fines for inappropriately disposed of industrial waste were enormous.

As they entered the boardroom all eyes were on Eli. The chairman, a tall, well-groomed man with sleek grey hair and a bullet shaped head, indicated chairs beside him for Eli and Olga. Olga's cousin Stefan Cusack who was seated across from them raised an eyebrow in greeting.

Eli had never accepted that the experiment to produce the first revolutionary new fuel which had resulted in a disastrous explosion near the Caspian Sea had been the cause of his son Boris' deformity. Olga had been staying in Kazakhstan with relatives and Boris had been born just after the explosion.

Eli was not an imaginative sort of man. Even learning that the toxic emissions had resulted in large numbers of children being born with deformities in that region he did not suppose for a moment that they were anything to do with Boris' deformity. He knew enough about political intrigue to know that figures could be rigged. Politicians and activists had always used such facts to restrict the growth of profits to industries when it suited them.

"We welcome Mr Jampolski and his wife," began the chairman of the company, "but fear we do not have pleasant news. The disposal of all waste products from the production of our new fuel will have to be stopped immediately." He took a sip of water and paused as though waiting for Eli to grasp the significance of what he was saying." The Russians have stopped our funding until we can prove that our waste management strategies can pass the stringent laws now coming into force. We shall have to conduct a survey into sites in Scotland before we can assure the Russians that their own sites will be safe." He paused again and looked searchingly across at Eli. "Can we have your report on the sites in this area?" he said, tapping impatiently on the table at which everyone was seated.

"I can assure the Board," Eli began tetchily, "that security on my sites is beyond reproach."

Just then the fussy little man with the sandy hair got up, went over to the chairman, and whispered something to him.

"Unfortunately Mr. Jampolski," said the chairman, "the information we have is that there was an explosion from recent deliveries to your own site in Kilkune only last night."

Eli stood up white and inwardly shaking with rage while giving the outward appearance of politeness and calm. He had been too well disciplined by his father, as all the family had, to give way to physical displays in public.

"Mr. Mannheim sir, that is impossible," Eli said in a deceptively calm voice despite the pallor of his face. "There were no deliveries yesterday. There was no one at Kilkune to authorise them. I was at the depot."

Olga glanced at Eli, and then at Stefan. Someone would be at the receiving end of Eli's fury. Stefan had had the good sense to work on this new project off shore, out of Eli's way.

"You understand if there has been a leakage that no possible recrimination can fall on the company. You and you alone must take the responsibility and suffer the consequences," the chairman said sternly." If we are to go ahead to finalise the production of this new fuel, it could revolutionise the way the world uses energy. We cannot be seen to be producing the same toxic effects that the oil companies are guilty of. We have to be seen to be above reproach. The world needs what we are on the point of successfully producing and the world leaders will be prepared to back us with capital if we stay clean." There was loud applause at this point from the rest of the gathering. "Mr Jampolski if it is true there are problems at Kilkune then you know the stakes. We will have to say we have never heard of you. We will have to cover our traces. You will not exist. I hope you understand."

From the committee members a roar of approval was heard. Olga looked at Stefan who averted his eyes.

Eli stood his ground and looked straight into the eyes of Mannheim, the chairman. "There is no possibility that what you say can be true," he said in an icy tone. "But If I am dismissed, mark my words I'll get even with the lot of you."

The chairman returned Eli's look with one of calm indifference. "If no one has anything further to say, the meeting is closed for the moment. I will discuss anything privately if you wish Mr. Jampolski. You know where to find me."

* * *

"What a complete farce and waste of time," said Olga, shouting above the noise in the helicopter's cabin as they flew back to the mainland.

Eli maintained a stony silence.

Once back on the mainland he suddenly gave way to his repressed anger. "I'll sort that lot out at the depot. Some heads will roll for this," he spluttered. "It's a plot Olga. How could the Environmental Agency have given the board information about a leakage last night at Kilkune when they are based in Strathclyde? Impossible! It's a personal vendetta and I'm going to find out who's behind it and when I do, I wouldn't like to be in their shoes."

"That new chairman, Mannheim," said Olga spitting with rage. "He sees the whole project as personal fame and glory. If Stefan and the other scientists pull this off it will seem to be Mannheim's doing. He'll get the credit and the profits. And where does that leave us? Where's the money to come from to keep up the castle and the estate? We've been pouring money into this scheme long enough."

"We knew the risks," said Eli, his tone hard and bitter.

"But we need money now Eli. This could be a real disaster. Already Mary is beginning to see how we've cheated on our tax returns. She's smart, too smart."

"She'll not give us away, not Mary."

"Don't be too sure. You're a soft old man with her. I don't trust her. I never have. It's time for our contingency plan. You knew when you invited the boy up what you intended. Eli. Remember, we need the money now."

Chapter 7

There was a knock at Davey's door.

"Davey," came Mary's voice.

Pulling his sweater hastily over his pyjamas he opened the door, and was immediately conscious of the sweet perfume that always surrounded her.

"An email for you…" She put a sheet of paper in his hand. "I took the liberty of making a copy for you."

"It's from Rob," he said, sitting down on the edge of his bed to read.

"Look, I'll leave you in peace to read it. Just thought you'd like to have it as soon as possible," she smiled, and turned to go down the steps leaving him alone.

'Hi Pol' he read, grinning at the familiar nickname. He'd hated his surname and the way some of the masters at school pronounced it, but his pals just called him Pol.

Thanks for the email. I can't believe all this stuff about you living in a castle. But that's what you said, so I'm sending this to Kilkune Castle so you'd better be there. I suppose you'll be expecting me to call you "Your Majesty" next time we meet. I hope that won't be too long. It's been a bit boring since you left.

But here's a bit of news you'll be interested in. Remember the old guy who gave out the prizes at last Speech Day? Well, according to Uncle Tom, he's a friend of the boss — they went to school together or something like that - and he's invited him up to your part of the world to do some fishing. I don't know exactly when but it's sometime before the end of the holidays, and Hughsie has asked Uncle Tom to drive him up there. So, you might get a visitor.

Uncle Tom says he's not staying with the old guy and Hughsie. He's staying at the pub in a place called Lochlan. He wants to do a spot of fishing himself. I'll give you the phone number at the end of this letter. I know you said you haven't got a phone there but I'm sure there are public phones — even in Scotland. You really must persuade that uncle of yours to get you a mobile.

Get in touch again when you can, and I'll let you know if I learn anything more.

Signed.

Rob Roy.......Just joking!

(Well if you can live in a castle I can at least be Rob Roy, or perhaps, Robert Bruce)

P.S. The number is 660012.'

Davey smiled to himself. Rob always thought he exaggerated things. This time though things were happening that even Davey couldn't have imagined, even in his wildest dreams. It was great news though to know that Uncle Tom was coming up to Scotland and since Billy had said there was a newly installed phone at the head of the loch that the local fishermen had been agitating about for ages he'd be able to get in touch. But Mary must have a phone herself. He'd ask her.

"You're looking mighty pleased with yourself," said Mary when

Davey came down to the breakfast already laid out for him in the great hall. "Sorry to dampen your spirits but I understand your uncle will be back shortly."

"Have I said Uncle Eli dampened my spirits?"

"Not in as many words. Guessed aright though didn't I?" she said.

Davey looked at her closely without comment and was startled to discover that round her neck she was wearing the very same amulet as the one belonging to his dead mother. What should he do? It was impossible. It couldn't be the same. He'd already locked it safely away. He couldn't blurt out anything outright, but he couldn't ignore it either.

"This, what you're so curious about," she said, conscious of his stare, and unclasping the amulet she handed it to him.

He saw on closer inspection that while it seemed to be exactly like his own, the clasp was different, and although both were made of burnished metal, this amulet had jewels set around the edge.

"It is…… I mean, I thought it was the same as …" he stammered awkwardly returning it to her.

"And is it the same?" Mary smiled, as she fastened it back round her neck.

"No, of course not. I didn't mean to suggest it was the same….." he broke off in embarrassment.

"As yours mother's, yes?"

"How could you know that?"

"You may be surprised what I do know Davey."

"I just know that my mother wore it all the time and I would hate to lose it. By the way there were some pretty weird people in the forest yesterday. I thought they were quarry workers but Billy said no. I wonder…….." Davey looked at Mary. "Do you know what they might have been up to?"

"Are you sure you saw such people? Strange thoughts can come to you in the woods, especially if you go deep into the ancient woods. Just being there can change your feelings and your thoughts. Perhaps this is what happened to you, you just imagined it."

"Billy was there too. We both saw their shadows although Billy was convinced it was a terrible monster called a Broch something. I definitely saw someone."

"Ah! Billy McGraw! He has a very vivid imagination and is a superstitious boy, just as many folk are in Kilkune. They imagine all manner of mysterious things."

"But we didn't imagine the explosion did we? I dropped one of the containers that were delivered yesterday when we took them down to the quarry. That wasn't in the ancient woods, that was real right enough."

It was clear from Mary's expression that she knew what he meant. Her light cheerful mood seemed to change and her face, usually so clear and beautiful, became suddenly lined and grey. It was as though she had aged a hundred years.

Davey gazed at her in horror. He had seen her sudden change of mood before but this was different. She seemed almost to wither and fade before him. He felt chilled to the bone. How could she be so many different people and have so many different moods? He looked away, frightened, and embarrassed.

Yet, when he looked back, intrigued, she had become the Mary of a few minutes ago. He was too taken aback to say anything and as Mrs Mcgraw came in just then to ask if he wanted any more porridge the moment passed, the opportunity was lost.

"Have ye heard when the master's due back Mary?" she asked.

"I believe they were delayed at the depot and couldn't get a flight to the island immediately which must have upset them a great deal. Mr.Eli never likes to be late for any of his appointments but he'll be here tomorrow or the next day at the latest. Which reminds me, I have to get over to Dunkeld to collect some papers and receipts for him. Will you be alright Davey until I return?"

"My Billy'll keep him company, don't fret ye self. And I think he's got some wood stacking to do. If ye call to mind his uncle left him plenty of work to keep him happy." Mrs Mcgraw chortled as she bustled off back to the kitchen.

Left to his own devices Davey decided that work or no work he was going to find out more about the mysterious folk in the forest.

Leaving the main door of the castle he hastened down the slope to the pine forest and was suddenly aware of a figure ahead wearing a red shawl. It could surely only be Mary. But she'd said she was going to Dunkeld. Perhaps she'd changed her mind, yet why would she venture into the forest alone? Nothing about Mary made sense. Her knowing about things before you told her anything, her strange moods, and even stranger changes of appearance.

If he followed her it would look as though he was spying on her but his curiosity won. He kept her in view without increasing his pace until she was swallowed up by the fringes of the forest and then he hurried to the spot where he thought she must have entered the forest.

There was a movement like a scampering of small animals and the same feeling as before that he was being observed as he entered the thickest part of the wood. There was no sign of the cheerful red shawl any longer. He began to feel afraid and wished he'd killed his curiosity and stayed back in the castle with Billy. Even chopping logs would be preferable to this cold eerie sensation of being watched.

The intensity of the feeling grew until he began to realise that he was not alone. He was slowly being surrounded by a group of men and women who had come up so softly behind him that not even a twig had been disturbed.

The women wore their fair hair braided around their heads and intertwined with flowers, while the men were dark skinned with dark curly hair.

"You are responsible for the *mal atmosfera*, no?" said one of the men. He spoke with a soft foreign accent which Davey thought might be Italian or Spanish.

"Excuse me?"

"What you call it? Poison air?"

Of course, thought Davey, they mean the fumes from the smashed canister.

"It was an accident. I didn't…don't know what was inside."

"But you are responsible," continued the man shaking his fist at Davey. "You spoil the air, kill the plants, the animals. You make *disordine*…disturbance in our rituals."

The man moved nearer and grabbed hold of Davey's arm. The crowd began to mutter.

"Let him go!" came a clear commanding voice. "He is not responsible."

The man let go in surprise as a tall young man with red gold hair, like a lion's mane waving and flowing down onto his shoulders, stepped out of the shadows. He wore a loose kind of tunic and a silvery band around his temples. His face was proud and he moved with a sense of his own majesty. There was such a profound feeling of inner quiet about him that all mutterings ceased.

"I am John Lotharion. You must be Davey."

Davey felt as though he'd entered some kind of parallel world or a world of myth, inhabited by wood sprites. How could this strange being know his name?

"Our leader, Theareo, is aware of you," he said as though he'd read Davey's thoughts. "You have unwittingly disturbed some very delicate proceedings…some rituals. They wish you no harm but you must not come here again. Do you understand? If you do, you must take the consequences and I will be unable to help you."

He turned and disappeared as if by magic and the group moving smoothly and rapidly was swallowed up with him into the darkness of the forest.

What had happened just now? Davey had been having some strange dreams since he came to Kilkune but this wasn't a dream. He went over the sequence of events. He'd followed Mary until she'd disappeared from sight, entered the wood at what he believed to be the exact spot where she'd vanished and then reality had turned upside down. Were these the same people's shadows that had terrified Billy and which he'd seen yesterday? And what had happened to Mary? Wherever she'd got to she'd clearly missed meeting that little lot. Why had he been forbidden to come here again? This was his uncle's estate. Who were these people? And who was their leader Theareo?

He walked back up the slope to the castle in time to see the black Mercedes drawing into the garage. Horrors! His uncle was back already. If he was quick he'd be able to get up to his room without being seen. He'd no desire to be confronted by Eli just yet.

He flung himself on his bed staring up at the ceiling wishing he was back at school, wishing he was anywhere but where he was. Gradually he became aware of raised voices and the sound of argument. He got up and opening the window peered out to see his uncle, Olga, Billy and his mother shouting at one another loudly. He was able to catch the drift of the hullabaloo.

"You had no right to move anything without my express permission," Eli was yelling angrily.

"An' I was only doing what I always does," Billy shouted back angrily defending himself.

"And you always were an idiot," said Olga joining in the fray.

"Ye don't go calling my son an idiot ye auld varmint." Mrs McGraw, red in the face, advanced threateningly towards Olga.

Then Uncle Eli yelled at Billy. "You can pack your tools now and leave." There followed a terrible moment's silence, and then Mrs McGraw could be heard saying stonily and distinctly, "If he goes, I go."

Davey saw her turn on her heel with as much dignity as her plump little figure would allow and both Billy and his mother disappeared from view.

"David!" came a furious voice.

Davey's heart nearly stopped, as he heard the ominous click, click of Eli's stick coming up the stairs. He couldn't avoid it, he'd have to face the music straight away. He opened his door and came down the steps to meet his uncle.

"Do you take your instructions from a daft servant and her half-witted son?" Eli shouted.

Davey remained silent looking straight at Eli. He had nothing to be ashamed of, he had acted in good faith. His uncle's eyes slid away from the boy's steadfast gaze.

Davey began to wonder how much his uncle knew already. Should he tell the truth now? Billy had said the damage and missing container could not escape notice. But there was no time to decide what to say. Eli, becoming increasingly irate, stormed on.

"How dare you sign for goods quite clearly addressed to me! Not content with that, you, and that worthless layabout McGraw, manage to drop one of the containers into the quarry."

"How'd you know...? Davey stopped, seeing the fury on his uncle's face.

"How did I know? I'll tell you how I knew. I was told in front of the whole committee who employ me. That's how I knew." His face was white with rage. *"Information has been leaked about an explosion at Kilkune"* is how they put it."

"It was an accident uncle. I didn't know the canisters were dangerous."

"You didn't know the canisters were dangerous!" roared Eli. "What do you mean, dangerous? Of course they're not dangerous." Davey was aware of his uncle's shifty glance.

"The one that I let slip accidentally, exploded and the fumes nearly choked us. So they must be."

"Oh must they, Mr. Know it all?" sneered Eli, who, beyond himself with rage, struck out with his stick catching Davey a blow across the shoulders. Davey didn't flinch. He had been taught by his father not to flinch when struck. "Stand up for yourself." Davey remembered him saying. "Never show anyone you're afraid of them."

This infuriated Eli further and with his free hand he struck him a stinging blow across the cheek, but Davey still stood his ground.

Sensing that he would infuriate his uncle further if he simply turned his back on him, he turned to go back up the stairs without a word, although inwardly raging.

"And you can stay in your room until sent for," said Eli clearly trying to take back the initiative.

After a short while Davey heard the sound of a key being turned in the lock in his door. It seemed all too familiar. This scene had been played out between himself and his father many times, even for small misdemeanours. His mother had wept and tried to intervene, but that had been his Dad's way, the way he himself no doubt had been disciplined by his father, Davey's grandfather.

The stinging cheek was not as painful to Davey as the realisation that with both Billy and his mother now gone, he was once again friendless and completely alone.

He bent down over the bed and drew out his hold-all. Opening it up he was horrified to see that the lock on the inside tag was missing. He felt inside the pocket, the amulet had gone.

Chapter 8

Davey had not stopped smarting - not from the pain of being struck but from the unfairness of his treatment. But he knew he wasn't going to give in, no matter how long his jailers kept him locked in his room.

He went over the recent events trying to piece together some of the strange things that had occurred. The missing amulet, from a locked inner pocket. Mary, knowing about his mother's amulet and wearing a similar one. The weird change in Mary's mood and appearance and the way she had just vanished in the forest. He was still convinced that the episode in the forest was not all in his imagination. Yet he wondered whether he really had been affected by the atmosphere of the place. Was he going crazy? "Sermons in trees and..." if he could only remember one of the quotations he'd learnt last term in English. He repeated the past tense of as many irregular French verbs as he could, finally deciding that he was in possession of his sanity.

His mind flitted back to life at Brentwood and he was just thinking of Rob's news about Uncle Tom coming to Lochlan when he thought he heard footsteps and a key being turned. Olga flung open the door and stood staring at him with hard, accusing eyes.

"Don't think you've been punished yet. There's work to do now the servants have gone. Down to the hall sharp."

Davey followed her, knowing that at the moment he had no choice. But all the time, in his mind, he was formulating a plan.

Olga took him through the main hall and into the kitchen where it was soon clear that the fire which heated the old fashioned stove had gone out and the one under the copper boiler which was used for heating water was also out.

Olga indicated a huge log basket that was empty. "Pine burns too quickly, drat it," she muttered, more to herself than to Davey. "You can fill this up with logs. Fetch a further basket and fill that, and then fill the buckets with charcoal. You'll find baskets and charcoal in the outhouse. You can then help me to light the fires, and when the stove is hot you can heat the fire bricks for the oven."

Davey had little experience of kitchens let alone one as ancient as this.

Looks like I'm going to have to learn pretty sharply, he thought, heaving the heavy basket of logs he'd collected from the outhouse. Trying to get the damp logs to light before piling on the charcoal tried his patience to breaking point. He marvelled at Mrs McGraw's endurance working in such an antiquated place. Poor Mrs McGraw. I wonder how they're getting on, he thought, wiping a charcoal-smeared face on his sleeve.

"Hurry up boy," said Olga sharply, cutting through his thoughts. "We'll never get the stove hot at this rate. You're not very bright. Use some of this old newspaper to get the fire going," she thrust the paper at him. "When you've done that there'll be the brasses to clean. They'll be waiting for you on the table in the hall."

Davey had never seen such an array of brassware to clean when he'd finally got the fires going. He was sure Mrs McGraw didn't have all these to do or she'd be working all hours of the day. Just where did he start?

He picked up the tin labelled Brasso and set to cleaning and polishing with black hatred in his heart. There's no way I'm staying here any longer than can be helped, he thought.

"Blast", he yelled as he spilt the sticky fluid all over the table.

Olga rushed in. "Idiot boy. You're as useless as that damn Billy. We wouldn't be in this mess if it hadn't been for your stupid grandfather and his inheritance…"

Davey looked at her in amazement, her face was purple with red blotches of fury etched on her cheeks.

"My grandfather's what?"

Realising her mistake and that she'd said too much Olga swiped the table with a cloth and left him wondering what on earth she could have meant.

His mind drifted as he wiped the residue up and he began his task again. Back and forth, round in circles. What did Olga mean about his grandfather's inheritance? What really was in those canisters? Why were the people in the forest so concerned about them? What rituals were they practising there, and who and what was John Lotharion and their leader Theareo?

So preoccupied was he with these distracting thoughts that he suddenly realised he had been polishing away at the same brass jug without noticing. As he glanced at it he became aware of his reflection in the smeared surface of the metal. It reminded him of Mary's scary transformation all twisted and unreal.

Then as he peered at the jug he heard a sound. He paused. Turning and looking up towards the gallery he saw a movement. Some one was watching him. Momentarily he saw a hand pushing through the wooden slats of the gallery. With a sudden realisation of what was happening he ducked, but it was too late. The heavy stag's head on its wooden plinth came crashing down and Davey lost consciousness.

Chapter 9

John Lotharion materialised in the midst of a pine forest on a Scottish hillside for the second time in less than a week. It was becoming more and more of an effort to raise the energy. Why couldn't the P.A.S. (Preservation of Ancient Sites) use the lesser deities for small jobs? Yet he had to admit the group of second century deities he'd brought over last time had proved very unprofessional in their behaviour, acting like a press gang with a completely innocent human. And now he'd been detailed to retrieve two of them who had failed to report back to headquarters.

He would have liked the opportunity to do something really big like the Brazilian rain forest or the Mexican and Polynesian sites. He drew a line at Hawaii though. It used to be such a peach of a job before all the tourists. They set up such hare-brained wavelengths that even as experienced a god as himself found it impossible to do an effective repair job on those sacred sites.

Scotland, he supposed, was preferable to the English sites. Take Stonehenge, for example, how could you work the old rituals to restore the ancient magic magnetic fields with so many half crazed humans trying their own brand of hocus pocus or whatever New Age fad was flavour of the week?

Even here in the ancient forests that had lain undisturbed for centuries the trees' energy fields were being interrupted by things like Tornado and Harrier low level practice flights, not to mention the spate of toxic waste which he was currently investigating with his boss Theareo. Oaks were in need of a strong infusion of determination, birches had almost lost their gentleness. As for the pines, their clear-sightedness had diminished immeasurably. One couldn't get a single clairvoyant idea out of a whole forest of pines these days.

John Lotharion felt he should put in for a 'residential' like the boss, less tiring than what he did dashing here and there. But then, she was a superior sort of deity and always came in for priority bookings.

Just then the tree beside him quivered and he caught sight of a black skirt, a red shawl embroidered with symbols, flowers and fruit and finally a pair of serious green eyes contemplating him.

"Theareo! We weren't due to meet until later," he said.

"No," said Mary wearily. "Forgive me for appearing in human garb but as you know changing from one form to another is exhausting work."

"Tell me about it. I've just been moaning to myself about the difficulties of working in this present era, but orders are orders and the P.A.S. was insistent on this particular task."

"I have already located seepage into the burn which flows into the loch. It is so bad now that even the locals are noticing something is happening. I am also concerned about the boy. His presence has sparked off new problems."

"May I respectfully remind my leader," said Lotharion slyly, "that Rule One of the Maxima Arcana states: The task of deities engaged in restoration work is to engage with the earth's energies only."

"Of course," said Mary testily, "but the boy is in serious danger, especially from the woman of the house, and above all he has managed to lose the amulet."

"The Polynesian deity amulet? How do you know that?"

"Come, come Lotharion. How do I know anything?"

"You mean everything don't you?" He grinned. "Well while that is serious enough you have to remember Rule Two: Deities of the ancient regime must not fraternise with humans.

"I don't need to be told thank you Lotharion. I know that we are expressly forbidden to get involved. *Working the kind of magic that involves speaking to their inner minds only when they are receptive makes our task the hardest of all.*"

Mary sighed deeply and Lotharion looked at her curiously. "*Taking on a residential has great risks doesn't it?*"

"*Yes, of turning into a human yourself and having all those troubling human feelings,*" she agreed.

"*In ancient times,*" said Lotharion, "*it was possible to have deep friendships with humans. Then people lived magically, lived close to us, and to nature. Now their minds are closed up like tight balls to magic and other worlds, or else they are so cock sure of themselves they think they know all the answers in the universe.*"

"*Yes, the modern human makes restoration work exhausting. But all this talk is self-indulgent. We need to re-assess our plans,*" she said in a more confident tone. "*Until we receive orders that the time is right for the final move we must continue as we are. Incidentally, you could make it your special task to track down the missing amulet. We shall need it. We'll meet again at full moon. Good luck with tracing your missing group members. We don't want them getting in the way.*"

Lotharion uttered a sound that appeared to be made by a chorus of voices chanting in harmony and then, he was gone.

Chapter 10

When Davey came to he was lying on a settee in the main hall. "Ow! My head," he groaned. "It hurts hellishly." His uncle was leaning over him peering at him curiously.

"Nasty accident," he said. "You're a lucky beggar. Luck of the Jampolskis. All you'll get is a nasty big bruise."

Davey knew it had not been an accident. He edged away from his uncle. The sight of his gimlet eyes boring into him sickened him. But the effort was too much and he sank back down again. The room swam before him.

The stag's head still lay on the floor, the tips of both antlers broken. One of its eyes had become dislodged and stared up at him in glassy defiance. He shuddered to think what might have happened had he been caught by those murderous looking antlers.

"Sip this." His uncle was forcing some liquid into Davey's reluctant mouth. Davey, distrustful of Eli's every move spat out the acrid bitter taste as soon as it touched his lips. He could still feel the foul burning sensation. Making a tremendous effort he propped himself up, but the effort only caused him to vomit violently and he lay back with closed eyes.

He thought he heard someone come in and start picking up the debris. Drifting in and out of consciousness he heard snippets of conversation, some of it in Polish.

"I think he's out for the count," Eli was saying.

"Now what?" This was surely Olga.

As Davey drifted in and out of consciousness he heard Olga's voice raised and angry.

"You know what we intended for the boy when you got him up here. We've got to get rid of him....... That inheritance...... It's ours by rights."

"How by rights?"

But Davey couldn't catch the answer.

"No!" Eli's voice was wavering now. "I told you ....it's too risky."

Startled by what he was hearing and only half understanding, his mind still fuddled, Davey struggled to come to.

Suddenly there was a loud knocking at the door.

"Now who the hell is that?" muttered Eli. "Olga go and see and get rid of them."

After a few moments Olga called, "It's Alistair from the village."

"What in the devil's name does he want?"

"He wants to know if he's allowed to take a group of tourists into the forest tomorrow do some divining for old wells and the like. And he'd like to do a quick survey now before they come."

"And how the blazes can he do that? The idiot. It'll be dark soon and he's almost blind."

"He doesn't use his eyes for divining, he uses a rod and his senses. Billy McGraw's with him."

Davey was by now much more alert and feeling a little better.

"Damned cheek, him coming back here," Eli yelled.

"Sh! You'll wake the boy."

"All right, just get rid of them and tell them to keep away from the quarries. For heaven's sake woman get rid of them before the boy comes round."

Now, thought Davey, before I lose my chance. He sat up abruptly and tried to stand but Eli grabbed him and forced him back down on the settee.

"Now my lad, we'll just get you up to your room where you can sleep it off. Come on now."

Loathsome as it was to accept his uncle's assistance, Davey had to allow himself to be helped up to the turret room and into bed. But he wasn't too far gone to notice that this time his uncle did not lock the door.

Left to himself Davey began to think rapidly. He wasn't going to get another chance to escape easily. He'd planned to escape through the little west window and down the cedar tree, but he wasn't sure how steady he was going to be. He tried to stand and fell back on his bed, he was far too wobbly.

I'd better wait for the right moment, when it's dark, he thought, but I hope there's a moon. Climbing down on a pitch black night could be lethal.

He tried to think what he would do once clear of the castle. If I make it, maybe I'll find someone, a solicitor, to help, he reassured himself. Then he was overcome with doubt. Who's going to believe me?

He had no watch, but his insides communicated very clearly that it was past suppertime. There couldn't be long to wait. He stuffed a notebook, Rob's email, and a few odds and ends he thought might come in useful, into his sports bag. He regretted bitterly that he would be leaving without his mother's amulet.

He lay on his bed watching the sky darkening over the silent hills and tree tops. He was beginning to doze off when he heard a small sound like something hitting the window. There it was again. Someone was throwing stones at his window. Still feeling groggy he stumbled over to the window. He saw Billy down below on the drive. He was pointing to something in his hand, but it was getting too dark to see what it was. Billy, turning his face up towards the window, began to mouth something. At last Davey realised he was saying "Is this yours?" He had to stop himself whooping aloud for joy. It could only mean he'd found the amulet.

A moment later he made out another figure coming out of the forest and approaching the castle. Davey recognised her by her bright red shawl.

In the space of a few moments Mary was knocking gently at Davey's door.

When Davey let her in she let out a gasp at the sight of his swollen forehead and the bruise which had now spread down over his cheek.

"What on earth's been happening?" Mary's face showed shock and concern.

"I think someone is trying to kill me. It was not my imagination and it was not an accident," said Davey in a carefully restrained voice, so as not to betray his plans to escape. "I've been sick but I'm feeling much better."

Reaching out her hand she touched his swollen forehead gently and Davey felt the pain ease wonderfully.

"I know your Uncle to be a rogue from what I have gathered already from his financial affairs, but seeking to harm his own nephew? Have you eaten anything since you were sick?"

"No nothing and I'm ravenous," Davey admitted.

"By the way, Billy found your amulet," she said, pressing it into his hand. "He guessed what it was from your description of it."

"Where was it?"

"Near the standing stones."

"Wow!" he breathed with relief. "But...How did it get there of all places? Mary...it was left locked in my bag."

"Billy came back with it, hoping to catch sight of you," she said quickly avoiding answering directly. "He says his mother insisted he came up with Alistair. She has been worrying about leaving you alone up here." Again she put out her hand and touched his forehead gently. Immediately Davey felt light, his head stopped throbbing.

"Now I'll just get the lie of the land, see what's going on in the castle. Stay where you are." she motioned to him. "You still look very pale. I'll be back as soon as I can."

✳ ✳ ✳

When she returned Davey was fast asleep clutching his mother's amulet in his hand. He looked so defenceless and, disregarding P.A.S rules about fraternising, she bent and kissed him gently on the forehead. She noted the sports bag by the bedside and understanding its significance, was filled with anguish, love and apprehension for his youth and innocence. She placed the bread, Polish sausage, and apples, which she'd retrieved from the kitchen, by the side of the bed. Her duties, she knew, were not to get involved but, as she had told Lotharion, this boy had become very dear to her. She could not directly change the course of events. Humans had to exercise their own free will, that was the law of the universe, but even if her knuckles were rapped by headquarters, she intended to keep watch.

Chapter 11

Startled by a noise outside his room, Davey woke and sat up in bed. The moonlight was streaming through the window illuminating the grey stone walls. His head no longer ached and when he stood he began to feel stronger. He listened carefully but could hear nothing more. He placed the amulet safely inside the zip pocket of his bag and noticing the food remembered Mary's visit. He took a bite of one of the apples. Half way through the second bite, he froze.

There was a distinct sound of something being shifted outside his door. His body became rigid with fear. When at last he dared, tremblingly, to open the door he caught his breath in horror. He gasped. Beneath his feet gaped a yawning abyss. The largest stone, which formed a kind of landing outside his door, had been up ended. Davey knew that old castles had booby traps of all kinds to ensnare enemies but this was not a castle that went back into those far off days of feuding between clans. The stone seemed to be hinged like a trap door.

That settled it. He quickly zipped on his anorak, opened the window and threw down his sports bag, praying that the sky would remain cloudless and the moon bright while he was climbing down the cedar.

He climbed on to the window ledge and tried to grab hold of the nearest branch. How easy it had seemed in the daylight and how near.

Gritting his teeth he lunged out and grabbed the branch with both hands. He swung there for a horrible moment, stabbing out with his foot trying to get a foothold, back and forth, back and forth. Damn, he thought, his arms aching, trying to find a niche. Pushing away foliage and twigs that grazed his hands he began inching slowly and painfully along the branch which flexed with his weight, until he could at last grab hold of the trunk.

Wow! He breathed a sigh of relief as he wedged one foot and transferred his weight over to the trunk. For the moment he was safe. He had no idea of the age of the tree or whether any of the branches were rotten but trusting to his intuition, he felt his way down branch by branch, thankful for the brightness of the night and the strength that he felt oozing into him as he saw the ground getting nearer and nearer.

At last! He jumped clear, still a bit shaky, but free. Picking up his bag Davey set off at a run, making for the forest.

The forest was an eerie place at night. There was the strange scurrying of invisible nocturnal creatures. Trees creaked and seemed to have voices of their own. Things unseen crackled under foot. Only glimpses of moonlight sifted through.

Davey swore as he bumped into prickly bushes and hard tree trunks. He tried to orientate himself. He had jumped from the west window and had followed a line that should come out at the southern end of the loch. This surely, was the route he had taken with Mary. But would it lead him away from the main quarry road? He caught his breath. What if he fell into one of Eli's pits?

I'll just have to keep on going down hill, for about an hour, he reasoned, pressing on. Eventually he caught the sound of a stream, a burn, as it was called by the locals. He remembered such a burn and realised that it was soon after that when they came to the quarry. He knew he would have to veer away from the path to avoid the danger of toppling over into it.

Then through the stillness of the night there came a distant pulsating sound. At first Davey could not make it out, but as it grew louder and less muffled by trees and bushes he was sure it was the throb of an engine, a car engine.

He forced himself to lie quiet for a moment and to listen intently, even though his heart was beating furiously.

There were intermittent glimpses of headlights through the trees. The car had to be travelling along the old quarry road and heading towards the loch road.

Half crawling, half stumbling he reached a kind of scree. A single rolling pebble could set the whole slope careering off, creating a din that would echo for miles. His heart in his mouth at this new kind of terror, he balanced like a circus performer carefully watching his step. The moonlight was brilliant now, illuminating his every move. At last he reached the edge of the slope in safety.

He was just congratulating himself, when he slipped, sending a shower of pebbles hurtling down the hillside. The enormity of the sound was incredible. He knew whoever was in pursuit of him could not have missed it. He began to run, not caring where he stepped. He was now in deadly earnest. The noise of the throbbing engine grew louder as he raced on with bursting heart, his breath coming in gasps. Then there was silence.

The engine had been switched off. The headlights disappeared.

Could they, whoever they were, be following on foot? He lay face down in a clump of heather. His head swam and his tongue felt as though it was on fire.

He tried to make out distant shapes but everything looked menacing in the half-light. He could have sworn he saw something move. Davey, galvanised into action shot out, racing headlong towards the loch. Suddenly he felt himself falling, scraping rocks with arms and legs as he hurtled down. He landed on a narrow ledge, looking up at the steep slopes of a quarry, where he lay winded but miraculously unhurt.

A voice above him called, "Don't move. I'm coming down."

Looking up, Davey was aware of long hair that even in the moonlight gleamed with reddish gold. Eventually a long slender but firm man's hand grasped Davey's. "Can you stand?" said the voice of John Lotharion.

Cautiously pushing up against the rock face Davey stood.

"Your other hand now," commanded Lotharion. "Steady now, push with your feet against the side as I pull you up."

The strength yet gentleness in the sure control he felt in Lothario's hands was something Davey knew he would never forget.

At last Davey staggered and collapsed onto the heather at the top of the quarry. He lay back and looked up at his rescuer speechless with relief.

"Thank Belarius and Lynea not me," said Lotharion as Davey tried to utter his thanks. He turned towards a man and woman whom Davey recognised as part of the group he had seen in the forest. "They followed your trail. Lucky for you and for them. Perhaps their punishment may not be so severe now as they've saved you and your precious amulet."

But before he could ask Lotharion to explain what he meant there was a distant squealing of brakes and a stomach-churning thud.

* * *

Mary was the first on the disaster scene. She had just finished her report to headquarters detailing the return of the missing members of Lothario's group with an exonerating clause concerning their rescue of the boy and return of the stolen amulet.

Now she was surveying the wreckage of the Mercedes. Altogether, she reflected, a sorry night's work. Both Eli and Olga had survived a headlong plunge off the quarry road down the burn side that flowed into the loch. Why Eli had been driving without headlights and coasting dangerously down with engine switched off she preferred not to think about. Right now she needed to get both safely to hospital before either of them bled to death. Eli's injuries were not as severe as Olga's but she'd survive. In her role as human employee she knew she was allowed to do whatever was required. In these circumstances she was not infringing the rules by performing a humane act even if she carried it out by magical means.

And besides, she reflected, Eli and Olga would never have the slightest knowledge how they had arrived in hospital on the night of full moon, fifty miles from home.

Chapter 12

Davey found himself at daybreak alone by the loch side. There was a thick mist over the loch and his face and hair were wringing wet. He ached everywhere and felt as though every bone and muscle in his body had been damaged. He remembered very little of the previous day or night. It all dissolved into a massive blur when he tried. He seemed to remember that he was running away from someone. Then his brain clicked into position as everything rushed back. He'd had an accident.

I've got to find a telephone, he thought.

In the damp chilly morning air his shivering reminded him that a warm fire in a local pub was perhaps what he needed more than anything. With his bag slung over his shoulder he headed off, skirting the edge of the loch, hoping the mist would lift and that someone would come along to give him a lift.

There can't be much chance of any traffic at this hour in the morning, he thought desolately. Then he heard the rattle of a milk float as it trundled out of the mist and pulled up along side him. The milkman who was doing his early morning round between Dunkeld and Lochlan peered hard at him.

"Where ye heading laddie?" asked the bearded young man "Haven't seen ye in these parts before."

Davey thought he looked at him suspiciously and knew that it must be unusual to see a boy out alone in mist at this time in the morning with a bruised face and torn anorak.

"Can you drop me at the pub in Lochlan? I'm meeting my uncle there," said Davey, hoping he sounded plausible.

"Hop aboard then. Ye're lucky 'cos that's where I'm going."

Davey was glad that the float clanked and clattered so loudly, or rather that the milk bottles did, as it slowly made its way round the loch, for it made conversation almost impossible. Fortunately the young man did not attempt to query him further, although Davey thought he looked suspiciously at him once or twice.

They drove into the small courtyard of a pub called appropriately "The Angler."

"Well here ye are then. I'll wish ye well wi' finding yer uncle."

"Thanks again," said Davey watching as the float rumbled away.

What on earth am I doing here? What am I going to say? He stood for several minutes without a thought in his head.

A young woman wearing an apron and carrying an armful of bottles came out into the yard.

"Can I help ye?" she said, as Davey stood there making no move.

"I was hoping to meet my uncle here, Tom Smithson. I think he's booked for a few days stay."

Like the young milkman she said nothing at first. Looking at him a little warily but giving him the benefit of the doubt she directed him to the front door of the pub. As it was still very early the door was firmly locked but she'd clearly passed on the message and after much unbolting of locks and turning of keys, the landlord in open necked shirt and dungarees let him in.

"If it's Mr Smithson ye want then I'm afraid you'll be sore disappointed laddie. He's no expected until the end of the week."

On seeing Davey's downcast face the landlord said, "Now see here ye look half starved and I wouldna' be surprised if ye havena' walked some way. I'll ask ye no questions, till ye've supped. Just come into the lounge and Kirstie'll make ye something to eat and we'll soon have the fire going in yon grate."

But Kirstie, the young woman whom he'd met in the yard, did want to talk. She wanted to know where he was from and why his parents hadn't checked before letting him set out. Was he running away?

Davey countered at first with the fact that he had no parents and as the landlord entered at that moment he saw an unspoken question pass between the two.

"Ah well, Kirstie, the boy's famished, questions later," said the kind landlord.

Davey was just tucking into a bowl of steaming porridge when he heard a loud knocking at the front door.

"At this time in the morning," said the landlord bustling away. "Whatever next!"

Davey could hear men's voices. He hoped no one would come in. Then he heard the landlord say, "We've heard and seen no one just a stray lad, but he's no from these parts."

"It's the police," said Kirstie, coming into the room with a plateful of toast for Davey. "There's been some accident over at Kilkune. The old man's car's a total wreck but they say," her voice dropped to a whisper, "there's no body. It's a mystery, plenty of blood but no body."

Davey shivered.

"The police are going over to Kilkune now to make enquiries. Somebody must know who was driving the car and what happened." Kirstie was clearly excited and bent over Davey in conspiratorial fashion. "There are strange goings on at Kilkune, very strange. I wouldn't be surprised if that old man up there hadn't planned it all for reasons of his own." She tapped the side of her nose knowingly.

Davey's sharp intake of breath caused her to look at him with some concern.

"Now look at the laddie, and me frightening him to death wi' these tales."

But Davey's concern was more for the fact that soon the police would connect a missing boy with the night's events. Hopefully there was no one who would report him missing. He was grateful for the help he had received but he ought to move on. No one must suspect that he was connected with the castle at Kilkune.

"I should be going," he said. "I will pay you for the food when my uncle comes, but I should be going now."

"And where'll ye be going then?" said Kirstie, looking at him anxiously. "Do ye have somebody we can phone ?"

"No. No, thank you, Kirstie." Davey thought of the Laird, but he didn't want to get him ringing Brentwood and causing a stir. He hadn't the faintest idea what he was going to do, when the phone in the bar began to ring insistently.

"Stay here, while I answer that," said Kirstie, crossing over to the bar.

"I'll just ask him," she was saying into the phone. "Would your name be Davey?" she asked. "It's someone wanting to speak to Davey."

Wondering who could possibly know where he was Davey picked the phone up gingerly. "Yes?"

"Mary here. I need to speak to you urgently. I guessed you'd be there."

"How?" Davey began and then gave up. Nothing was happening that made any sense, and Mary was being as mysterious as ever.

"I'll be over in less than half an hour. Wait for me in the yard at the front of the pub"

* * *

Fortunately when Mary arrived Kirstie and the landlord were busy in the back sorting out receipts and delivery dates for the following week, so there were no awkward questions to answer. She didn't say much as she and Davey drove off together except that his uncle and Olga had been in an accident and had been transferred to hospital.

"But how could they... where were they?" There were too many questions flooding his mind.

"It's time you were put in the picture," she said eventually. "I know why you ran away. And yes it is hard to believe your uncle intended you harm. We both know he's a greedy and unscrupulous man but..."

"But I'm his nephew," Davey broke in. "Why would he try to kill me? Was it something to do with Olga? What have I done to cause them to hate me so much?"

But Mary remained tight lipped staring straight ahead and suddenly he noticed they were not going in the direction of Kilkune but driving through a valley he hadn't seen before.

"Where are you taking me?" Davey sat up in alarm.

"You have to trust me Davey. Believe me I am your friend."

"And Eli's?" he said bitterly.

She turned to look at him clearly surprised by his tone.

"If you know so much about him why are you still working for him. You knew about the pollution and all the poison waste didn't you?" He ranted on unable to stem the hurt, the sheer bewilderment of everything that was happening.

Mary pulled to a halt where a nearby burn rushed down the over boulders and stones. Davey got out and Mary followed. She gestured wordlessly to him to follow her.

"No, thanks. I'm walking back to the pub."

"Very well. But first can I ask if you still have your amulet?"

He hesitated and felt round his neck where he had fastened it after being rescued by Lotharion. He nodded but turned away.

"If you can't trust me then trust the amulet your mother left for you."

Davey turned round and saw that she was walking up a path away from the burn to where a curious circle of stones stood out among the heather.

A feeling, like the same sense of awe that he'd had when he saw the standing stones in the ancient wood came over him and he walked towards them. He stood silently for what seemed a long time trying to remember something, something important.

"What is it Davey?" asked Mary, gazing at him intently.

He looked at her puzzled, unable to make sense of what he was feeling. He had the strangest sensation of being swept back to another time, another place.

Mary beckoned him inside the circle and it was as though time was standing still. He hardly dared to breathe, it was the weirdest sensation. "It's as if I've been here before," he murmured. His eyes suddenly felt heavy and his head swam.

"Not here but somewhere in a far off land, far away in the Pacific Ocean," came a voice, which might have been Mary's, but it was all echoey and hollow. "When you were only a tiny child your mother dedicated you to a special task decreed by your ancestors, and it is now ready to be performed. Your uncle has been involved in a very dangerous project, the manufacture of a new type of fuel. In the wrong hands it could destroy huge areas of the earth."

The voice ceased and then from far, far off came another voice. "The moment has come for the decree to be enacted, for the boy to be given his task."

His eyelids grew heavier and heavier and finally closed as a gentle voice lulled him into a sense of tremendous calm.

As if he was in a vision he began to watch a scene unfolding. At first it was as though the place was filled with the sound of native people chanting.

Then a deep silence came over the crowd as they knelt in turn before the altar of their nature god.

The stone god beamed down at them with a wide smile, his head wreathed in flowers, and in place of his beard were sheaves of corn.

Among the crowd was a young woman. She was clearly Polynesian, with dark skin and hair, but she was wearing western clothes. She was carrying a small child in her arms. The child had her dark skin but, astonishingly blonde hair. As she approached, a priest stepped forward and she turned to smile at an older European man who was standing apart from the crowd. He returned her smile with one that was amused, almost mocking.

As the young woman knelt before the priest she leaned forward, placing the child in his arms and, taking a necklet or amulet from around her neck, placed it on the child's forehead.

"Aya," said the priest, intoning her name, "as you were given this precious amulet of the Acholiwai by your forefathers and as you are bound to fulfil its purpose, so you in turn must pass it on to your son when your time comes to return to them, and his moment to act comes."

The old priest laid the child before the altar, dedicating him to the service of the god who beamed down from his wreaths of flowers and sheaves of corn."

The vision faded and Davey, in his still drowsy state thought he saw a new image of a land full of the cries of torn and dying birds and mutilated animals. Landscape after landscape seemed to roll before him blackened and charred. Skeletons of trees stood out starkly, mutely against a lurid sky.

Then a curious feeling like emerging from an underworld came over Davey as a mist fell, shrouding everything. When the mist cleared Davey saw his rescuer John Lothario and with him Belarius and Lynea from his group. But Mary, where was she?

In her place stood a beautiful figure in gauzy robes of shining silvery hues. There was a transparency and brilliancy about her appearance that was so dazzling the light almost hurt and at first Davey was unable to recognise her. Wound round her forehead and her long corn coloured hair was a silvery band like the one Lotharion wore.

Davey breathed the name "Theareo", knowing instinctively now who Mary was.

Chapter 13

There were five at the table that evening, Billy McGraw, Mary, John Lotharion, Davey and of course Mrs McGraw herself. Since neither Mary nor Lotharion ever partook of human food there was plenty for those whose appetites were young and healthy.

Mrs McGraw had prepared a special feast. There were candles on the long dining table, glasses ready for a toast, steaming tureens of homemade soup and a casserole of rabbit and homegrown vegetables.

Both Davey and Mrs McGraw had grown accustomed to Mary's strange habit of not eating, but Davey did wonder if Mrs McGraw might be offended by Lotharion turning his nose up at her excellent supper. But then, everyone was in such good humour, and it certainly didn't seem to offend her.

"I understand that yer uncle is making good progress after the accident," said Mrs. Graw beaming as she dished out second helpings to Davey and Billy, "although ye might be a wee bit sad to hear that Olga is only making a slow recovery."

Davey glanced at her but she had a completely straight face, except that her eyes had a mischievous twinkle in them. No one made any comment. With Mary acting temporarily in her employer's stead, Mrs McGraw and Billy had taken up residence in the castle and seemed to be thoroughly enjoying life.

As for Davey, glancing around the table at all of his friends, he felt like the lord of the manor and could almost be said to be happy, except that he now knew he had a secret he couldn't share with Billy or his school friend Rob.

At times he felt elated, thrilled by the idea of being specially chosen for an important task. But there were other times when he felt terribly alone and terrified, not knowing what might lie ahead.

Mary proposed a toast to Mrs McGraw for her resourcefulness in providing the meal. Davey saw her round open face was wreathed in smiles. Then there was a toast to Billy for restoring the lost amulet, and to Davey for his courage. Everyone there had their own understanding of the events of the last few days and it did not enter the honest but simple minds of Mrs McGraw and her son to puzzle things out too deeply. It was enough that they had a job to do, to look after Davey while his uncle was in hospital.

✻ ✻ ✻

Much later that evening Mary, as Davey still preferred to think of her, Davey and John Lotharion sat in the small upper room that Mary called her office. It was lit by no lamp, yet it was as bright as daylight.

"Acholiwai," she was explaining to Davey, "was not only the nature god of the ancient Polynesian culture but his image also now serves as the emblem for all things linked with preserving natural life. Some cultures call him one thing and others yet another. Perhaps he is best known in the West as 'The Green Man.' He is also," she said, taking off her amulet, "a symbol for the Committee Lotharion and I serve and whose duties are to preserve ancient magical sites throughout the world."

Since the day in the glen Davey had tried several times to ask Mary about the meaning of the visions he had seen but she had avoided answering him until today.

"Owning this amulet," she said pointing to her own and to Davey's which he now wore around his neck on a chain Mary had given him, "is of great significance. It means you are ready to devote yourself to the task of restoring the ancient power sites of the planet." She paused to give Davey time to consider what she had just said. "In fact," she continued, "there are only three such amulets in existence. There may be imitations, but only three that contain the power to restore the natural vibrations to the magical sites."

"Did my mother know this?" he asked.

"She certainly knew that owning the Acholiwai amulet was both an honour and an obligation."

"Why didn't she tell me?"

"Perhaps she felt you were too young."

"But she left it behind." The full implication of this slowly began to seep into Davey's mind. "And.........she always wore it."

"Perhaps, she knew you would find it when the moment was right. There is always a right time for things to happen.

"You never told me how it disappeared from my room."

"Members of my group," broke in Lotharion, "thought to take matters into their own hands despite knowing we must not directly interfere with human affairs."

"But it was locked securely and hidden under my bed. How could they have...?"

Lotharion smiled serenely but gave no answer.

"Tell me," asked Mary, "what did you see in the glen in the circle of standing stones?"

"My mother holding me as a young child, a priest and some sort of ceremony."

"Yes, that was your dedication to the service of Acholiwai."

"I saw my father. He wasn't taking part though."

"Your father's own background inclined him to be very mocking of your mother's culture."

"Was that also why she never spoke to me about it? I know my father often flew into a rage with my mother calling her stupid and silly."

"People only do that when they don't want to understand another person's beliefs," said Lothario. "It's often quite distressing to think that everything you have ever believed is being challenged."

"Did you see anything else Davey?" asked Mary very gently.

Again Davey heard the heart rending cries of a thousand creatures, saw their death struggles, felt their pain, smelt the acrid smoke of burning, saw blackened desolate fields and no people. The land was empty.

"Do you now understand?"

There was a long silence. Davey was still struggling to know how the second vision related to him when Lotharion spoke.

"In the past there were sacred sites from which man drew his energy and connection with the Great Spirit. Now the whole balance of the earth depends on restoring this natural energy."

"Magic builds up in some places," said Mary. "It accumulates naturally in the wood of certain trees, in isolated and ancient woods. There is a great store of magic in this place, in Kilkune."

"And you're saying that Uncle Eli is destroying it with the waste he's storing in the quarries because it's seeping out into the loch and everywhere," Davey suddenly broke in.

"Yes," said Mary.

"What my uncle has been doing is wrong, but why do we need magic? Don't we have stronger kinds of energy now?"

"High technology and high magic are all the same thing," Lotharion explained. "In the past magic required long training and carried with it the responsibility to use it wisely for the good of the tribe." He paused and Mary gave Davey a penetrating look. "Without that it became destructive, evil. The same is true of modern technology, and all modern uses of energy."

"The amulets I spoke about have as much power as anything in your modern science but, like anything powerful, only in the right hands," said Mary gesturing towards the amulet Davey was wearing around his neck. Davey trembled as she said, "You, Davey carry the insignia of Acholiwai. We know you are the one to use this power and carry out his decree. We cannot decide for you. You do not yet know what is involved or how dangerous it is likely to be."

Both Mary and Lotharion were again silent. Davey's heart was racing. His thoughts scattered, when suddenly Lotharion drew out an amulet from under his tunic, and placed it in front of Davey then pushing Mary's towards him, said "They are yours . Take them. You will need them in your task. Their power is equal to anything your century has ever known."

Davey hesitated. What was he really being asked to do?

"Your task is to prevent your uncle's involvement in a project from becoming the frightening reality of the nightmare vision you had in the glen."

Davey looked wildly from one to the other. How …….?

But, before there was any answer, before the amulets could be put away, a sudden strong gust of wind filled the room. There was a violent flash, then darkness.

Chapter 14

Davey shuddered. He felt an intense chill. Something had entered the room and was moving in the blackness. He held back the desire to scream.

Here! What the devil's going on?" came Billy's voice as he hammered on the door, shattering Davey's terror. The light in the room returned as quickly as it had been snuffed out. Lothario opened the door to find Billy with a tray bearing a now extinguished candle, a jug of apple juice, and three glasses.

"That was one hell of a d...draught," he said setting the tray down in front of Mary. "And, if ye don't mind me saying so, one hell o... of a stink."

"All right Billy," said Mary taking the tray from him. "It was a poor dead bird that got dislodged from the chimney by the draught. Can't think what might have caused it."

Billy went out shaking his head and wrinkling his nose at the smell.

"I didn't see any dead bird. What was it?" asked Davey shivering after Billy had gone off muttering to himself.

"That was a small demonstration of how nothing will stop the powers of evil from manifesting where there is an unguarded source of such infinite power within its grasp," said Mary.

"What do you mean?"

"That was Satrydon," said Lotharion. "An old trickster, arch enemy of the P.A.S."

Davey noted the warning glance Mary shot at Lotharion. What was she trying to keep from him?

"It's nothing for you to fear while we are with you and while you are wearing the Acholiwai amulet," she said, gathering up the amulets. "The Acholiwai amulet has the power to protect you and give you strength."

Davey was suddenly overwhelmed with a feeling of great sadness. He bent his head and hid his face. Why then had his mother left such powerful protection behind? Did she know she wouldn't return and so couldn't keep the protection any longer but was bound to pass it on? How terrible to know in advance that your time had come. That was bravery, the sort he was sure he would never be capable of. He blinked back his tears.

"The green emeralds," continued Mary, looking at him with some concern, "have the power to give guidance and this," she pointed to Lotharion's amulet edged with red rubies, "offers solutions."

As Mary pressed the red and green amulets into his hands Davey felt a tremendous surge of energy shoot through his entire body. Shocked by the sudden impact he let the amulets drop on the table in front of him as though they were live coals.

"Their charge will not harm you only energise you," said Mary

"You have no need to be afraid," said Lotharion. "You have just witnessed how powerful they can be. Such power carries its own danger and can be a magnet for evil but only if you don't know how to use it."

Davey looked at him incredulously.

"If you knew the danger…why didn't you safeguard them? And why, if you know so much can't you…?"

"Because," Lothario interrupted with a shrewd smile, "you have to see for yourself. What would be the point of telling you without showing you what could happen? As deities we are bound by certain rules. We are not allowed to alter the course of human destiny until we find one who is ready to act for the good of others and has the courage and willpower to do so. But that has to be his own decision. We can only watch and guide from afar."

Mary again pressed the red and green amulets back into Davey's hands. "They're yours… if you choose."

She took down a folded sheet of paper from a shelf behind her, spreading it out on the small table.

"Here is a detailed map of the Mannheim operation your uncle Eli is involved with on the secluded island of Torksay. And here," she pointed to a central shaded area, "is the key to the manufacturing process of the new fuel. Only the scientists engaged directly in the work have access. Olga's young cousin, Stefan Cusack, is a key scientist. It is through him that you will have to find out what to do."

Davey's temper suddenly flared. How dare they just assume that he was going to play the role of hero. "No way! I'm not having anything to do with any relative of Olga's," he said firmly, "or any plan my uncle might be involved in."

"Do you really think you have an option?" asked Mary. "Consider very carefully before you decide. Think why your mother left the amulet for you to find."

"She left it hoping I would find it and realise it was a good luck symbol," said Davey.

"Oh, Davey, Davey, have you forgotten so quickly the first vision you saw?"

It was just that, he thought, a vision, an imaginary vision, like a daydream. How could he be sure it had really happened? Mary and Lotharion seemed capable of creating anything they wanted. Was he really destined to undertake such a dangerous mission as they had suggested? How he longed at that moment to be back at school, back on the playing fields, back with Rob and his mates, larking about. He wanted to shout 'prove it to me then, prove that I am the one who has been chosen to do this'.

"We can't prove it to you," said Lotharion guessing his thoughts. "We can only ask you to listen to what your heart is telling you. Ask why we all carry this sacred symbol. Ask whether you want to turn a blind eye to what the man who claims to be your uncle tried to do to you and will still try to do to the land around us."

At which point Davey nearly gave in but there was still the question of Olga's cousin. How would anyone who was working with Olga and his uncle agree to help him?

"That's not a problem," Lotharion said, accurately reading Davey's mind. "Stefan is a scientist and lives totally for his work. I doubt very much whether he has ever considered the moral implications behind the fuel he is helping to create. Did the scientists who created the hydrogen bomb? What do you think? Stefan he is not fond enough of Eli to be worried whether he helps his nephew or not."

David shook his head. "I'm still sure he won't want anything to do with me."

"Your task," said Mary ignoring his remark, "is to find out what synthetics they are using and whether the factory can be dismantled."

Davey let out a gasp, "How on earth….?"

"They will not suspect a mere boy of spying," she interrupted.

"Mannheim has conducted illegal enterprises in other parts of the world," added Lotharion. "The P.A.S. has a damning file of his activities from destroying tracts of rain forest in South America in search of fuel compounds, to digging up valuable historical sites in Mexico with the same aim. So far he's got away with it. But he doesn't know that we have been waiting to trip him up. You, Davey, have given us that opportunity."

Lotharion, folding his arms, sat back in his chair waiting for Davey's response.

Davey looked doubtfully at the amulets. "I don't begin to see how I can do this."

"We can contact Stefan Cusack and ask him to look after you in his island quarters while your uncle is in hospital," explained Mary.

Davey looked alarmed. "Is that safe? What about Mannheim?"

Mary smiled. "We know all about his connections with your uncle and with the waste spillages in Kilkune," she said, "and, will make this known unless he lets you stay with Stefan."

"I think that's blackmail, Mary," Davey grinned in spite of his doubts. "What about your non-interference in human affairs?"

"Indirectly it is interference as you call it, but it will be you who will be the human agent."

"I haven't said I will." Davey paused, struggling hard to push down his fears. All he wanted was to get back to school, never to see Scotland ever again, never again to hear the words Acholiwai or Green Man. He was afraid he wasn't going to be up to it. On the other hand he was being trusted with a tremendously important task. As he touched his mother's amulet he felt her love for him and a renewed strength and confidence surged through him. He knew what he had to do.

"Well?" asked Lotharion.

"I'm going to need lots of help."

"Good boy, we will be working behind scenes, helping you every step of the way."

Davey's mouth felt dry, his throat still tight and as he reached for one of the glasses of juice he couldn't help noticing that the other two glasses remained untouched. He couldn't resist asking why, except for the well water at table that night, he had never seen Mary touch food or drink."

"Even in our human form we live on light and air," she explained. "We are made of completely different matter and are nourished in different ways from you."

"It is difficult for humans to imagine four or even five dimensions and impossible to grasp the idea of a sixth where matter becomes distilled into pure energy or light," said Lotharion, "and which we have learnt to bend, making ourselves visible or invisible, as we choose. We can also use the speed of light to transfer ourselves to wherever we are needed. The amulets can do this too, but only in certain circumstances."

Mary smiled at Davey's look of sheer disbelief. "All things will eventually evolve to reach this same stage, but it needs considerable change of heart in the case of humans. It looks as though you may be thousands of years behind," said Mary, glancing at Lotharion.

"There was a moment when it might have happened," he said. "It was the millennium. Everything was poised for a great change to occur. In the spirit world the message had gone out that humans were ready. The force of Shambala was unleashed, but then there was a cataclysmic change in the rotation of the spheres in the tenth world. The force of change began to slow down and things began to return to where they were."

"Except," said Mary, with a knowing glance at Davey, "that certain humans began to wake up to realise things they had never understood before. Unfortunately some of the new knowledge which was prematurely released was not at all helpful for the world and some is still being used for selfish and destructive purposes."

"Meaning this Mannheim and my uncle, I suppose," said Davey.

"Among others," Mary rose to her feet. "Take the map with you Davey," she said, dismissing him. "We have work to do now. Tomorrow Lotharion will go over the plan with you and show you how to use the amulets. I will arrange your flight with the heliport, and will contact both Mannheim and Stefan." She turned at the door. "Sleep well, Davey. Remember to wear your protection at all times."

"You have a great day ahead," said Lotharion as they both left.

A great day. What could he know about Davey's idea of a great day? The thought of the next day filled him only with the same sort of apprehension as school exams or a visit to the dentist. There was no way he was going to sleep. Yet in spite of his fears Davey felt strangely energised, if only there wasn't this peculiar churning in his stomach.

Going down to the great hall he found Billy reading a newspaper. On a small table by his side was a glass of what looked and smelt suspiciously like something stronger than apple juice.

"Don't know how you can see in this light," Davey said. The candles that had been used for the meal were guttering and almost burnt out.

"Ye get used to it. Says here," said Billy,"that there's p...problems with p...pollution in the lochs and streams in some parts of the Highlands. It don't seem they understand what's c...causing it. It's going to be a p...problem with the trout fishing I dare say."

"Do you feel like a game or something, that is if you can still stand?" asked Davey.

"Och, it's nothing but a wee d...drop of stuff Ma keeps in the k... kitchen, it wouldn't hurt a fly. Can't play computer g..games in this stinking old place but I tell ye what though. Old Alistair, the chap in the village who does a' that w...weird stuff I told ye of, g...give me these." He took a pack of cards out of a drawer in the table. "Don't know quite how it w...works but there's some instructions here. Want to p..play?"

Davey sat down looking at the cards that bore pictures of Greek gods and goddesses and heroes that he recognised from books he had read. Billy struggled with the book of instructions.

"C...canna make much sense on it. Look ye I'll spread them all out face d..down an ye can choose one. The b..book'll tell us what it means."

Davey carelessly picked up a card and handed it to Billy.

"It says," said Billy reading aloud slowly and hesitantly, "Ye canna make up yer mind b...but it's too late now to go b..back on things. Go on p...pick another."

Davey obeyed tremulously, picking up another card.

"It's like a t...tower all crumbling," said Billy, looking at the card and turning the pages of the booklet to find the answer. "It don't rightly say exactly b...but it's something about everything around ye changing forever. Wow! Ye d...don't seem to be having much l..luck. Try another."

"This is the last. Your turn next," said Davey. He stretched out his hand, picked up the card and handed it to Billy.

Billy looked at it and whistled in dismay. "And I'm n...not showing ye this. We'd best stop it."

Davey snatched at the card but Billy held fast. "Ye're no seeing it."

"Come on you can't believe in such things. It's superstition after all."

"Ye asked for it then." Billy threw the card down on the table.

The card showed a figure in black robes, his face hidden beneath a dark helmet and the word printed above was ... Death.

Chapter 15

After a hasty breakfast the next day Davey met Lotharion in Mary's office.

The unearthly glow of last night had been replaced by a cold grey light filtering in through the small high windows of the room. Lotharion, his flamboyant red hair severely tied back, pig tail fashion, gestured to Davey to sit by the table where he began to unfold a plan of the Torksay operations.

"Ready Davey?" he asked.

Davey nodded, some of his bravado of last night was beginning to evaporate.

"Anyone visiting the island," said Lotharion, "would see a small helicopter landing pad, a few dwellings and, close by, the sort of meeting hall you might find anywhere where there is an isolated community." He paused, adding, "Nothing there to arouse suspicion?"

Davey waited. Where was the witty, vivacious Lotharion? He seemed to have become a priest or teacher.

"Look!" He pointed to the plan. "This shows the centre of the operations, which lie hidden underground."

Davey looked at the plan, which had numbered sections, and an explanatory key in the bottom left hand corner.

"And that's where I'm going to have to go?" Davey frowned

"Learn the plan by heart, the entrances and the exits. I'm afraid it won't be plain sailing, even when you've learnt this."

Oh, that's really great, thought Davey, and aloud he said "You said you'd help."

"If you're in any kind of danger you can summon Theareo or myself through pressing the amulets. Calling the name Acholiwai will bring help from your ancestors."

"Lotharion.......," Davey began. He wanted to say, "I'm not sure, suppose I can't go through with this?" He was hearing Billy's voice "Ye canna make up ye mind but it's too late now." Was he really such a ditherer?

"What is it Davey?" Lotharion's voice was no longer teacherly.

"Last night I played a game with Billy. It foretold something really scary. Then there was that Satrydon. It was like an omen."

"Depend upon it Davey those things only have power if you believe in them." Lotharion's eyes twinkled.

"There was this prophecy in 'Macbeth'," said Davey as the remembrance of the part he'd played in the school play flashed into his mind, "Two truths are told...as... prologues to the swelling act."

"And," said Lotharion, smiling broadly now, "what caused the prophecy to come about? Wasn't it Macbeth's own belief and his over active imagination?"

"Wow! How did you know that?"

Lotharion tapped his forehead significantly. "You'd be surprised what we know."

"But what if I fail? What if I screw things up?"

"Trust the amulets, take courage, and you'll not fail. The

knowledge is deep and secret. Today I can give you only the barest of hints, but you will learn quickly as you begin to live with them and observe them."

He asked Davey to hand him the ruby and emerald amulets. "Perhaps you noticed yesterday," he continued, "that the gems changed in brilliance whenever a question or problem was raised." Davey had not but he intended to observe them now more carefully. "There are also other ways you can pick up clues from the amulets. Use your other senses of smell, hearing, and touch. Ask the emerald amulet a question, Davey, while holding it in your hand. Shut out all distraction, keep your mind still. Don't try too hard just keep the question clear."

The question that came to him was whether Mary had already started the plans for his journey to Torksay. He kept the idea clear without allowing himself to think of his own fears, just holding the thought steady, steady, when he was aware of the most delicious smell of woodland flowers and then the salty tang of the sea.

Lotharion looked at him and smiled. "There you are. It was easy wasn't it? You thought about Theareo. Try it again, but not too hard, just relax. Does it tell you more?"

Davey pressed the emerald again in his hand and felt an icy cold shaft slice through his chest. At that very same moment there was a knock at the door.

"Quickly," said Lotharion, "put the gems out of sight."

But it was only Mrs Mcgraw coming to take away the tray of drinks from last night.

"What you just felt was a warning to you to keep the gems secret," he said when she had gone.

"You must remember to keep the emerald on your left and the ruby on your right. Stay alert. Keep asking and making careful note of what the different sensations mean. It isn't difficult really, the power will flow through you anyway. All you have to do is to trust and connect, just connect with the power."

"My mother's amulet, how do I use that?"

"Just think what it means?"

"You mean it protects me and gives me strength?"

"Yes, and it will communicate with you. It will speak to your heart, not audibly but you will hear, you will know what you are being guided to do. Your ancestors will communicate with you and you will begin to learn how there are communications everywhere. Even trees and rocks communicate at their own level. For humans there is always a strong communication with their ancestors but, Davey, you must be patient and learn to hear them and speak to them."

"Are you saying I can really speak to them? How?"

"Press the amulet, visualise seeing your mother's eyes, listen and you will hear them. They have chosen you. Ask if you need their help. Believe me this is no fantasy, this is real. Good luck, Davey," he said placing the rolled up plan in his hand. "Don't let anyone know you have this plan or speak to anyone about these things."

* * *

"What's Stefan like?" asked Davey, as Mary drove him to the heliport.

"I haven't met him in person but we have his dossier. He is single, younger than Olga by many years. He seems to have been looked after by her as a young boy when Eli was working on a fuel scheme in Kazakhstan. The resulting pollution caused many deaths and untold damage. Today the Caspian Sea and surrounding area is an ecological mess due to fuel companies and enterprises like Eli's having no proper waste management schemes. Many fish and land creatures have become extinct, crops have suffered, large areas are derelict."

"Were Olga and Stefan with him?"

"Yes. Olga, who was pregnant at the time, always blamed Boris' disability on Eli's disastrous scheme. Stefan would have been too young at the time to have been aware of such things. Today you will find he is a man fanatical in his pursuit of science."

Just facts, thought Davey, which don't really tell me anything about him. "I just can't see anyone who's related to Olga wanting me to stay."

Mary said nothing more. She wanted to ensure that Davey understood what he had to do.

"You need to observe and describe to yourself exactly what is going on. If you can, find out more about the materials being used. You must trust the amulets to guide you and to take you to the heart of the operations."

"I thought you said the fuel they're making is dangerous."

"It is. It could spell disaster for the world."

"I don't understand anything you said about the materials. Oh! It's just pointless my trying to make sense of all this."

"Don't look so puzzled," she said smiling at his bewildered expression. "All we need is for you to witness and observe, come back and report what you've seen in detail. We are strictly forbidden to do this ourselves which is why you have been given the task."

"And the materials are……..?"

"The materials are composed of highly crystalline stone only found in areas where there is intense magnetism. Such stones act as condensers where huge untapped energy gets stored. Mannheim's team has discovered a process to tap this energy and it is this that is tampering with the delicate balance of the earth."

"So was my uncle quarrying materials as well as depositing waste?"

Mary smiled the secret smile that Davey had seen before but she did not reply.

It seems I'm on the right track, he thought. "I never understood what you meant by saying Uncle Eli was rich."

"Kilkune and the whole area is a rich source of natural power. When Eli discovered this unfortunately his greed and carelessness were on the point of endangering the whole project. The last thing Mannheim's group wanted was publicity and anyway Eli was no longer an asset to them. They were near to mastering the process, and had all they needed for completion of it."

"And my uncle, who it seems, had invested a lot of money into the whole scheme would be ruined if Kilkune's power was no longer needed?" said Davey beginning to put the pieces together.

"Exactly. If he could no longer exploit the natural wealth of the estate, that meant serious trouble, he was already deeply in debt."

"And if this man Mannheim has now found out how to complete the process he can move on to find other mineral sources elsewhere?"

"That is what we fear."

"So how can he be stopped?" asked Davey.

"That's in your hands. At first you will just spy and keep alert. Be precise about what you see and hear. You will need precision if you are to be believed when you return."

If I return, he thought, as a queasy feeling hit his stomach.

"As they now have only a finite supply of materials, a disrupting of the process, or," Mary's voice became almost sinister, "a destruction of it…" her voice tailed off as she concentrated on a sharp bend in the road, "would be perfect."

Davey glanced sideways at her. Her wide grey eyes held something more than concentration, and he felt there was an indifference in the way she spoke to him. Here he was, probably heading for a huge disaster and she didn't seem to care. She was talking to him in a matter of fact way, as though he was a stranger. Mary, who had been at times so protective of him, was giving him his marching orders in a cold and uncaring way. She had become his sergeant major, nothing more.

He longed to be with Rob or Billy, someone more his own age, someone who didn't make any demands on him. The amulet round his neck suddenly began to feel warm and a very gentle movement like a stroking sensation could be felt. It was as though the tender fingers of his mother were soothing him as they had done when he was younger and couldn't sleep. At once he relaxed and set his mind on the task ahead. He must put personal things out of his mind. He was going to do what ever was needed and he was going to succeed.

Mary loosed one hand from the wheel for a moment and touched his shoulder. The gesture was slight and lasted a mere second but at the same time the pulsating sensation of the emerald signalled quite clearly to him that Mary was thinking the same thought.

The airfield was minute with only a single storey shed. Two other people and a child were waiting for the flight. There were a couple of planes out on the field that looked not much bigger than toys.

"Stefan will be waiting for you," said Mary, handing Davey his flight ticket. "He's expecting you to stay two or three days at the most. I have said I will be in touch about Eli's progress in hospital and that you will be no trouble."

As soon as the helicopter came in Mary turned to leave. There was going to be no farewell. Davey put his hand in his left pocket and clutched the emerald, which immediately became warm and melting like a sweet gentle caress. There was no need for him to doubt Mary's affection for him. He just had to learn other ways of knowing things from now on.

Chapter 16

Soon they were airborne and Davey, who had never flown in a helicopter before, was amazed at the delicacy and grace of the way it rose straight up from the ground. The deafening rattle and roar within the cabin made it impossible to steady his mind and think of what lay ahead.

He watched the coastline disappear and saw small islands ringed with foam come and go beneath them. Then, ahead, he glimpsed a white beach. The sea looked amazingly shallow and clear. He could see dark green fronds of seaweed, and the dunes on the shore looked like children's sandcastles. Now they were coming down, landing on a small strip of tarmac. There were no buildings of any description in sight, and only two men were waiting by a small wooden fence. He had no time to think which might be Stefan. He grabbed the small rucksack Mary had loaned him with his few possessions in and, walking down the steps that had been lowered from the helicopter, gulped in the warm air coming from the still whirring blades and at the same time mingling with it came a cold, fresh, salty sea tang.

As soon as he and the other passengers were clear of the noisy whirring, a small thin bespectacled man came up to him.

"David? I think you're David," he smiled, and Davey heard again the familiar Polish rhythms in his voice. "Sorry to hear about your uncle. Is this your only baggage?" He looked pointedly at Davey's rucksack. "Bare essentials, yes?"

"I've got a book a friend lent me and a compass to use on the island. Oh! And a pair of swimming trunks."

"Won't be needing those unless you've got a skin like a rhino. The sea's freezing at this time of year, or any time as far as I'm concerned."

They followed a path which skirted the white sandy shore through scrub and tall reedy plants and grasses until it sloped deep down into a valley or hollow where there was a huddle of rough stone houses.

"I'm afraid there isn't much to do here and I'll be working late most days but, come on, let's drop your things and then you can see where you'll be living while you're here."

In the centre of the valley was a long hanger like building.

"This is where we all eat together," said Stefan. "Don't often get visitors, so you'll find us a bit rough and ready. And this is where I live." He took Davey's arm and led him through the door of a stone cottage, which seemed to be squeezed thin and narrow by the row of cottages either side of it. It was dark and smelt musty inside as though it wasn't much lived in.

"There's one tiny bedroom you can have, upstairs on the right. It's not much to look at. You'll have to wash in the kitchen. I have a radio in here and a computer you can use if you like. We do keep in touch with the mainland by radio in the main building. So that's it. After the evening meal you and I can do some catching up."

Davey decided that Stefan wasn't scary like Olga. In fact, he quite liked this small shy man. He went up to see his bedroom and looked out of the stamp-sized window. The valley rose up on the far side where he saw boulders and overhanging craggy rocks. The small centre of Torksay would be hidden from the sea and, snuggling down under the lea of the rocks, might be difficult even to spot from the air. Davey emptied the contents of the rucksack Mary had packed for him onto the bed. There was a change of underwear, a clean T-shirt, swimming trunks which he'd put in at the last moment, a small torch, compass, the Mannheim map of the operations centre and two packets of biscuits and a book.

He was eager to see what the book was she said she'd put in for him. It was very old and the pages were coming away at the seams. The title read "The Nature of Gemstones". It didn't sound very exciting. Thankfully there was electricity, so he'd have a chance to check on his map and look at the book later as it was already beginning to get dark.

The refectory or dining area in the main building was buzzing with the noise of different languages and the clatter of cutlery when Davey and Stefan arrived for the evening meal. White-coated scientists were helping themselves to plates and utensils from a serving hatch and then serving themselves from huge bowls of food laid out on tables at the far end of the room. Davey noticed the young couple who had been with him on the flight. The woman waved at him cheerily. He wondered how everyone could behave so normally and whether they had any idea of how dangerous the project was they were working on. Didn't they care? They were talking together as though they were engaged in the most innocent of occupations.

"Are they all foreigners?" Davey asked Stefan as they helped themselves to the food.

"The group over there are the only English speaking people here," he said, indicating the young couple Davey had met on the flight, and two older scientists. "Mannheim, our chief, has gathered here scientists from all over the world. Today is a special visitors' day, but most of the families live too far away to visit."

"They must miss their friends and families."

"Yes. It can be a lonely life, but when you're engaged in something so new and exciting it's all you think about."

Stefan's eyes shone as he spoke and Davey remembered that Mary had said he was a good scientist but not particularly good with people. He wondered if he had any family apart from his cousin Olga.

"Visitors are usually only allowed to stay twenty four hours anyway. It's surprising that Mannheim has allowed you to come for longer. He doesn't often make exceptions for anyone."

They sat down at a table set apart from the others when Davey noticed a tall man with smooth grey hair making for their table.

"Here's the chief himself coming to speak to you," said Stefan.

"This must be David, Eli's nephew." The hand Mannheim offered Davey was cold, clammy, like touching a toad thought Davey as he looked up at a pair of coldly glittering eyes.

"Stefan looking after you all right?"

"Yes thank you," said Davey, shuddering as he caught a gleam of hostility in the man's eyes. Of course he didn't want him here.

"Enjoy your stay," was all he said as he strode off. Then he stopped at a distance and beckoned Stefan to him. He seemed to be speaking to Stefan with some urgency but Davey was too far away to hear what was said. Instinctively he knew he was warning Stefan to be careful.

Mannheim spoke briefly to another scientist who looked up and glanced at Davey and then, going to the dark wooden panelling at the end of the room, touched something that caused the panels to slide open. For a brief moment Davey glimpsed another room beyond, and then the panels slid back together.

Afterwards they strolled back to Stefan's house. It was dark, but the sky was brilliant with stars. Such a brilliance Davey had never seen.

"The skies out here can be awe inspiring," said Stefan following Davey's gaze. "You're right out in the open sea. Nothing between. Just you, sky and sea. But it can get bitterly cold out here at night. Let's go in, you're shivering." He placed a kindly arm round the boy's shoulders.

"By the way I shall be out early tomorrow, but I'll leave a note of the times for the meals and a key to get into the main building if you happen to miss any of them."

"So the main building is kept locked at all times?" As Stefan did not seem to hear him Davey was left wondering why it was locked if there were only project workers on the island.

"We all work different hours and often have to help ourselves to food," said Stefan pushing open the door to his cottage. The kitchen staff will not be on duty if you miss the scheduled times so you will have to eat whatever you can find."

Once inside, the cottage was warm and cosy. "No problem with heating," said Stefan grinning. "After all, that is our speciality here."

Stefan settled himself in an easy chair. "Your uncle's secretary," he began, as he poured a glass of vodka for himself and lemonade for Davey, "must be very persuasive. Mannheim wouldn't readily agree to letting you stay unless…….," he broke off, tipping back the vodka in one gulp, "he thinks you know something about Eli and it's better to have you here under surveillance, as it were."

Davey said nothing.

"Well, do you?"

"What do you mean?" asked Davey, evasively.

"How much has your uncle told you about our operations here?"

"He has told me nothing, nothing at all," which was perfectly true.

Stefan poured a second glass of vodka. "You probably know your uncle worked on a similar project many years ago in Kazakhstan."

"Mary, his secretary, told me something like that."

"I know he's your uncle but he never really liked me. Olga, looked after me when I was very young, but Eli always made me feel I was in the way."

"Me too," said Davey. "I think he hates boys."

"He became a bitter, twisted man after Boris died. That first project was a disaster in more ways that one. Now we know much more than they did then. Success is almost ours. Hopefully there's nothing now that can go wrong. Must not go wrong. After what happened to Boris I am determined there will be no mistakes. All the safety checks will be checked and double checked." Stefan's face was becoming redder and he seemed to be becoming chattier the more he drank.

Sensing it was the right moment Davey asked, "Are the laboratories where you work in a different part of the island?"

But Stefan wasn't as drunk as that. "Ah! Now that's a secret," he tapped his forehead mysteriously. "But we don't need large premises. That's what's so marvellous." Stefan, unused to being listened to, warmed to this intelligent and interested boy. "One drop of 'agent magenta' could power a whole factory for a year. That's the beauty of it you see David. It takes months of work to produce the smallest of quantities of the "agent". The wastage is out of all proportion to what is produced but the result. …." Davey could see the excitement in Stefan's eyes. "The cost of producing such a minute quantity is very high now, but ultimately everyone will clamour for it and who knows what that could mean. The storage is minimal. No huge power stations. Those will be things of the past."

"But isn't it dangerous?"

"All scientific inventions can be dangerous. Look at the hydrogen bomb. Look even at the motor car. It kills more people than those killed in the wars going on in the world. It depends on who's controlling what, how it's used. That's Eli's job, Mannheim's. They're in it for the power; me, for science's sake."

"Don't the scientists have a say in how it's used?"

"What we are into is a scientist's dream," said Stefan choosing not to reply. "Vast power in the tiniest of containers." He smiled a dreamy, far away smile as he continued to drink. "Of course there are risks but think of the huge leap for mankind. It will bring untold benefit to the planet…untold benefit. This time there'll be no mistakes…" his voice trailed off. Davey had ceased to exist for him. Gradually his head began to nod and he began to snore loudly.

Davey crept away to his bedroom and opened the book on the nature of gems. But he couldn't concentrate, unable to get the thought of how sincere and enthusiastic Stefan was. But then how could Mary be wrong? How could his vision be wrong? And hammering away in his head and pounding in his heart the instinctive feeling of horror and repulsion Mannheim had aroused.

Chapter 17

Davey decided to breakfast at the usual time, and explore later when there was no one around. If anyone saw him, he'd pretend to be having late breakfast or early lunch.

He went over to the table where the meal was laid out ready. A tall man with smooth grey hair was talking in clipped foreign tones to a man in a white coat. There was something familiar and yet ominous about the tall man. Then as he turned Davey caught a glimpse of his face and caught his breath, it was Mannheim. He was momentarily taken aback but then remembered Lotharion's words, "In certain circumstances the amulets can bend light and bestow invisibility."

Placing his hands in his pockets he touched both amulets gently, praying that this was the right moment. The next moment he put out his hand to take a bowl of cereals and a white coated woman scientist who clearly hadn't seen him stretched out and took the same bowl. Just then Mannheim turned towards him looking straight in his direction. There was not a flicker of recognition.

Not knowing how long it would take for the invisibility to wear off he made for the door grabbing a couple of bread rolls on his way out. Once outside he made a whoop of jubilation startling a group of seagulls that took off screeching towards the shore. It had worked. He'd actually become invisible. As his elation began to he fade he felt almost sickened by the enormity of possessing such power.

Deciding not to go back to the main building until he could be sure everyone had left, Davey followed the path that led to the shore. The sea was unusually quiet, lapping gently on the white sand. He picked up a handful of pebbles and threw them, one by one into the water, enjoying the plopping sounds they made. The silence that followed was so profound that he was filled with a sense of peace he had never experienced before. He felt if he stretched out his hands he might actually be able to touch it. There was no one in sight, only tiny birds playing at the edge of the sea, running in and out of the waves. As he approached them they flew off together in a swirling cloud of feathers. A spit of sand jutted out into the sea. Crossing it he found himself in a perfect little harbour. There was a jetty built up of rocks and stones and cemented together. Then, almost hidden by the dunes, he discovered a long wooden shed. Peeping in at the window he could clearly see canisters, like the ones he had helped Billy to unload, piled up high inside. So they must transport the waste products by sea and bring in the materials the same way, he thought. But there was no sign of a boat, only a little dinghy fastened with an iron hoop to the side of the jetty.

Thinking that it was time to go back to begin his reconnaissance he reluctantly made his way to Stefan's little house. It was very quiet inside and, putting his hands out to try to feel the same sensation he'd had by the shore, he stilled his mind and asked if this was the right moment to act. He immediately felt a burning sensation on his right. Taking out the ruby amulet he saw that each of the tiny gems was radiating as though on fire. The light from them was as brilliant as the flashing of a red traffic signal. It was the go ahead.

Lotharion, he thought silently, addressing him as he went towards the main building, how did I get into this? I feel like some kind of criminal.

"It's for a greater benefit than your own," said Lotharion suddenly appearing before him.

Davey nearly jumped out of his skin seeing the familiar, lithe, red haired figure. "Did I call you? What if someone sees you?"

"They can see me only if I want them to," said Lotharion. "You didn't directly call me but I sensed that despite your momentary success with the invisibility you were still having doubts."

"Doubts? It's like walking through a minefield. There's so much guesswork. I wish I was more sure of what I'm doing. How long does the invisibility last?"

"I don't think it is likely to happen again so you needn't worry. I can't easily explain it to you, some shift of light or heat perhaps. . .or the strength of your intention. But whatever you do, don't bank on it. The amulets are not the most reliable way of becoming invisible. And the effect is short lived."

Davey gave a sigh of disappointment.

"Don't despair. You are right on track. . . . ."

Someone was coming down the path towards them. It was one of the kitchen staff who greeted Davey with a nod and a curious look that clearly said, "Talking to yourself? Living on this island gets you that way."

"Lotharion?" Davey began when the man was out of ear- shot but there was no answer.

Davey sighed again, took the key out of his pocket, and went into the building. Inside it was eerily quiet, the sort that one feels in an empty theatre or school during holiday times. He went straight towards the panelling where he'd seen Mannheim slide the panels apart so effortlessly the previous night. There was no sign of anything to press, no display panel of coded numbers. He felt along the wooden doors and suddenly came across a raised knot of wood. The emerald amulet was sending out a buzzing sensation and as he took it from his pocket it flashed three times. Three must be the first part of the combination, he thought. Using his hands, feeling for the right sensation, he touched a spot on the panelling that was soft and yielded slightly to his touch. This had to be the place. Immediately the emeralds flashed four times, then twice and then three again. He tapped on the responsive spot, hoping that he would hit the right numbers - three, four, two, three. The panels responded by sliding open to reveal the second room he'd glimpsed last night.

At first he was elated by his success but it was quickly followed by panic as the panels closed behind him. He was locked in a room that was dim and windowless apart from a small skylight above. It smelt stuffy and stale. He was startled as a cobweb brushed across his face. Mustn't begin to get jittery, he told himself.

Feeling around the walls he touched something hard like metal that made him jump. In the dim light he could just make out a sort of lever in the shape of a dragon's head. According to Lotharion's plan there was an underground tunnel leading off from this second room down to the centre of the operations.

The dragon's head might open a door to the tunnel, he thought. He pushed it, tried twisting it and pulling it but the lever would not budge. Then he heard voices and saw the panelling beginning to slide open as light filtered into the room from the restaurant area.

He prayed fervently he was still invisible as two white coated scientists passed within a hairsbreadth of him.

"All the checks were in place. It's the first time we've had power problems," one of them was saying, but neither paid any attention to him. It was as if he had frozen into the atmosphere or become part of the scenery.

Davey watched as one of the men placed his fingers into the

empty sockets that served for the dragon's eyes and a door slid open in the wall. He had a momentary glimpse of a tunnel lit with a strange kind of fluorescence. Then the door closed and he was left alone in the dimness of the room.

Now he knew the way down to the underground area that appeared as a shaded area on Lotharion's plan. He was about to follow by trying out the eye sockets on the dragon's head lever when he heard muffled voices and knew that some one was coming out of the tunnel. Quickly he hid behind what he took to be packing cases and in the red glow saw Mannheim and the man he'd been talking to at breakfast emerging from the tunnel. He watched as they approached the panelling. This time although it was too dim to be sure, Mannheim seemed simply to place his hands on the centre panel and it slid open effortlessly, closing noiselessly behind them after they stepped through.

Davey waited until he felt the coast must be clear and pressing his hands on the centre panel found it yielded to his pressure easily.

That's quite enough for one day, he decided as he emerged. And with beating heart and racing pulse he rushed back to Stefan's house and safety.

By late afternoon Stefan still wasn't home and Davey, tired of reading, went for a walk along the beach. He heard the helicopter land and take off again, no doubt taking the day visitors back to the mainland. He watched as it grew smaller and smaller on the horizon and then all sound ceased. He felt again the incredible silence surging back, broken only by the piping sound of an oyster catcher and the mewling of gulls. He began to feel homesick for Brentwood, for Rob and even for Billy and Mrs Mcgraw. He sat down on a clump of marram grass staring out to sea. Several metres off shore he saw something resembling a shiny ball bobbing in the waves, then there was another and then another. He stood up shading his eyes from the glare of the still strong light of the sun as it began to sink below the horizon. Then he realised that they were heads, animal heads. At first he thought they were dogs swimming out there. He went down to the edge of the water intrigued. Then he saw the fins, as with unimaginable speed and grace three sleek grey bodies sliced through the waves towards him and he knew they were dolphins. They were waiting for him. One, the largest, raised its snout, opening it to reveal sharp white teeth. He could have sworn it was smiling. Taking off his trainers and rolling up his trouser legs, heedless of the coldness of the sea, he waded through the waves towards them. He stretched his hand out to touch one of the round grey heads. The creature nuzzled him as a small friendly pony might and gazed up at him with round soulful eyes. Then the three of them turned and swam into deeper water looking back at him, inviting him to follow.

They swam back, nuzzling him, making gentle echoing sounds, nudging him, causing him to open his legs as to his great delight they swam playfully through them. The sun was sinking rapidly and as the light faded the three sea creatures gave him one last friendly push and were off once more leaping, freely soaring into the evening air.

Davey watched, full of the most incredible delight, until they were no longer visible.

He spoke to no one at the evening meal. Everyone seemed occupied with his or her own affairs. They were talking together as if something was causing them concern.

He returned to the cottage, and toyed with the idea of sending Rob an email but wondered how he could avoid saying what was happening to him. Instead he listened to the sports' programme on Stefan's radio until it was time for the news before going upstairs. He lay on his bed thinking about his meeting with the dolphins, wondering whether he would ever see them again. Staring up at the ceiling, thoughts began to whirl round in his head. He was unable to forget that underneath the quiet beauty of the island some fearful thing was being made.

Then he heard Stefan gently opening the door.

"Are you awake Davey?" he asked softly. "Sorry to have left you all day but there's a big panic on."

"What?" asked Davey, sleepily.

"One of the generators is playing up and we're working overtime to try to keep on schedule. If we can just get enough power to keep going for the next few hours we're there, home and dry." Davey could hear the thrill of excitement in his voice. "It's tricky though. If the power does fall below the critical point the whole process could be in serious danger."

Davey was fully alert now. He knew what the success of this project meant to Stefan. He also knew that time was running out if he was to succeed in his task.

"Sleep well. See you in the morning," Stefan said. Then, just before he closed the door, "Oh! By the way, thought you'd like to know. Your Uncle Eli is out of hospital. He's fine. Been out now a day or so. Got the news this afternoon."

"Great," said Davey his heart plummeting.

Davey lay, outwardly still, but his mind was racing. He mustn't let this news distract him. Would Eli try to find him once he knew he was missing? "Focus," he told himself sternly, "you've got to focus."

He waited until he felt Stefan must surely be asleep, slipped out of bed quietly, and looked out of the window. There were no lights in any of the other windows in the settlement. Taking the torch, he checked the underground operations on the plan and crept downstairs carefully.

Soon he was outside, taking deep gulps of pure island air. Then he caught the familiar sweet fragrance of woodland flowers.

"Mary," he gasped.

He could not see her but he heard her voice clearly. "Beware of the third gate," was all he heard. If it hadn't been for the scent he would have thought he'd imagined it.

"Mary," he whispered, half to himself, "Mary, I'm so afraid."

But the only sound was the distant breaking of waves on the shore.

Taking a deep breath, he touched Aya's amulet round his neck reminding himself to stay alert. Then he set off not knowing what or who he was going to meet or what exactly he was going to do. Although he knew Mary and Lotharion were never far away he wished he could see them, talk to them.

Panic began to set in and a sense of guilt. This was Stefan's dream he was about to destroy. Stefan who lived for his work and who had been so kind to him. It didn't feel like the greatest thing in the world any more. He longed to go back to his room and pretend he'd never heard of Lotharion or Mary. Fear erupted inside. If it's so important, why me? A question he'd asked himself before.

At that moment the moon came out and shone brilliantly down making everything look so beautiful. He remembered the grace and beauty of the dolphins. It was as though he was being reminded where Stefan's dream could lead. Science was capable of creating wonderful things, but if it was misused, and in the hands of a few who might use it for their own ends, then they could destroy the beauty he had found on this lovely island. He'd just have to go on. The amulet round his neck gave a sudden jerk as if in agreement.

Gritting his teeth in determination, he unlocked the door to the main building.

Chapter 18

The main building was in darkness. He waited until his eyes got used to it, not daring to risk using his torch in case someone saw it. Gradually he was able to make out the outlines of tables and chairs by the light from the star-filled sky shining through the window. He made his way to the panelled doors feeling for the slight knot in the wood and the spot on the left. He held the emerald amulet close to it and sure enough the gems winked three times, four times, twice and three again. As he tapped in the code the panels began to slide open, closing noiselessly behind him as he went through.

Should be safe to use the torch now, he thought. He moved quickly over to the wall feeling for the dragon's head and turning his fingers round in the empty eye sockets was relieved to see the door slide open, showing him the wide tunnel and the strangely glowing red lights. As he stepped through into the tunnel the door closed with a slight click. The lights cast pools of luminous red colour on the floor of the tunnel which sloped down. While it was wide enough for two or three abreast the roof seemed to be getting lower and he was forced to stoop to avoid cracking his head.

Then he heard a distant tapping sound. He stood stock still and listened. It came again, an ominous click, clicking noise. His heart did a somersault. Despite his fear he felt compelled to discover the source of the noise. Hugging the shadows he crept closer until he could see two men ahead. Both were stooping but one was leaning heavily on a stick and his other arm was in a sling. Davey gasped, his worst nightmare was being re-enacted. He was alone, trapped, with no escape ahead. He was sure it was Eli, his worst enemy. He pressed his back heavily against the wall of the tunnel disturbing clouds of chalky dust. Almost choking, Davey clapped his hand over his mouth to stifle his coughing.

Panic stricken he looked around wondering how to escape. "Run, back," came an insistent voice from inside his head, but he knew he had no idea how to operate the door to the tunnel from this side. His fear paralysed him, his legs refused to budge. He was rooted to the spot.

He watched in terrified fascination as both men came to a grid-like gate with thick metal bars. Eli spoke into a panel at the side of the gate which swung open letting them through.

Davey willed himself to approach the gate. He couldn't give up now. His nervousness was heightened by the fear of being detected by an electronic eye. There had to be a password.

He took out the emerald amulet but it didn't flicker. He held it close to his ear listening carefully, one second, two.......... Nothing.

Then he tried the ruby amulet, listening intently for the faintest sound........ Nothing. He was suddenly angry. He hadn't come this far only to fail. And where was Lotharion who had last put in an appearance when he was least expected?

Then out of nowhere came an eerie whisper. It sounded like the wind whooshing in the tunnel behind him. "Sh...sh...aaa .sh....

shaa....." His stomach tightened and the hairs on the back of his neck rose.

"Sh..... shaaa......shaaa...d." There it was again.

Davey was terrified. He saw that both the amulets were winking furiously. Could that be the password? But it was too faint to hear. He moved to another spot straining to catch the sound but it was still too faint.

Perhaps the sound might be amplified if he could only get up a bit higher. He scanned the walls of the tunnel. They were craggy and in places jutted out. He put the amulets back in his pocket and, catching hold of one of the rocks which jutted out from the sides, he hauled himself up higher and listened again, his feet scrabbling for a foot hold. But still he couldn't catch the whole sound which seemed to fade out at the end of the word. He caught on a rock at an even higher level, using the one below to steady himself. And now the sound came clear and strong "Sh ...aadra...shaadra" That was so clear it had to be the password. He loosed his hand hold but found that his foot was skewing out of control, if he fell now he knew he risked breaking his ankle. He slithered with his hands, grazing them on the sides of the tunnel, and grasped a rock just as his foot slipped out of control. Looking down he knew now he was out of danger as he gradually eased himself back down.

Relief poured into him, confident he now had the password complete.

"Shadra," he whispered into the panel and the gate cranked open to let him through.

There were two ways to go. Should he go to the left or the right? He pressed first the ruby and then the emerald, the warmth on his left indicating he should choose that. He took the left turn which led round a sharp corner and he was suddenly aware of the red eye of an electronic camera flashing. He knew it was too late now to escape detection by trying to become invisible.

He would just have to go on. It could only be seconds now before he was discovered. Striding on, he found himself in a narrow corridor that led up to a long bare room glassed in on one side. The corridor appeared to continue into the distance.

I must be in some sort of observation gallery, he guessed.

Below him he saw a control room with dials and monitors everywhere displaying unintelligible graphics. There were white coated technicians on duty who were tapping in information on their keyboards. He caught sight of men in protective clothing moving in and out of a distant door. Could this be the third gate Mary had warned him about? According to Lotharion's plan this would be the processing plant itself and could probably be reached by following the corridor.

Suddenly one of the technicians below spun round in his seat. Davey thought he'd been spotted. But the man was talking animatedly to his fellow worker who came over to look at his monitor. Something was wrong. The display was flickering. The graphics were going berserk. A third technician joined them. A tinny electronic voice could be heard, "Condition critical…..' alert …alert… condition critical." The monitor blanked out. Then a second monitor, and it was soon apparent the whole control room was out of action.

Davey could feel stinging burning sensations from the amulets. He withdrew them from his pocket and saw they were emitting brilliant flashes of light. What was happening? Could their powerful radiations have caused a reduction in the power supply? Lotharion and Mary must have known this would happen. It was clear they had never meant him simply to act as a spy. He felt betrayed. But he couldn't waste time feeling sorry for himself. Stefan had warned what might happen if the supply failed. And soon, if not already, they would know there was an intruder.

He tore back down the corridor but the metal gate would not yield. He was trapped! He could hear the sound of voices behind him getting louder. Now more than ever he needed the guidance of the amulets. But before he had time to calm down a hand was clapped on his shoulder and he was roughly swivelled round. Davey found himself looking into the furious face of his uncle, and into the evilly, black eyes of Mannheim who held him firmly in his grip.

"What in hell's name do you think you're up to?" spat Eli, livid with anger. Davey winced as Mannheim's fingers bit into his shoulder like an iron vice.

A jarring sound could be heard, and a series of explosions rocked the control room as the door to the processing plant was blasted off its hinges. Intermittent lights flashed, alarms screeched. Intense scorching heat flung them backwards, forcing Mannheim to release his grip.

"What the devil?" yelled Mannheim above the piercing sound of alarms.

"We've minutes at the most before the whole thing goes up," screamed one of the technicians flinging a sweat-soaked mask off his face.

"Keep at it!" snarled Mannheim above the din. But panic had set in. Men were scrambling towards the tunnel while others were trying to find emergency exits.

In the furious heat, among clouds of dust from falling debris, no one except Davey saw Mannheim, with Eli hobbling after him, disappear through an exit. Swift as lightning he followed and, as the door clanged behind him he saw he was in a well-lit corridor. Some distance ahead of him, Eli was tapping impatiently with his stick as Mannheim shouted into a hand held radio. "Urgent request for helicopter, now. Without delay."

The next moment there was a huge explosion and Davey was pushed violently through an opening as if by giant hands.

Just for a moment he thought he must be dead. The deep purple of the night sky above was shot with thousands of shooting stars and brilliant jagged lights flashed before his eyes. Then he found himself rolling over and over, faster and faster, out of control, until his foot snagged on a root and he sprawled his full length on a bank of scratchy heather.

Severely winded, clothes torn, his leg bleeding profusely he was gasping in huge gulps of salt sea air. He could hear the noise of alarms and distant shouting. Looking back he saw the roof of one of the main building teetering crazily although the front part over the dining area looked intact. Jagged timbers were strewn over the forecourt. He looked down at his leg and felt sick. He knew he had to try to stop Mannheim escaping but dragging himself along the ground, because it was too painful to stand, was all he could manage. He was going to have to ignore the pain if he was to get help. And Stefan? His heart came into his mouth. He must get to Stefan. Surely he'd heard the explosion.

Then he heard the sound of a helicopter. It mustn't land. As yet there was no sign of either Mannheim or Eli but if the Acholiwai amulet was to fulfil its destiny it was now or never. He held it up in the direction of the incoming helicopter. The jewel gleamed brilliantly as it was caught in the glow of the moon. Nothing happened. The plane was now directly overhead and soon would be hovering over the tiny landing strip at the edge of the valley ready to descend.

"Shadra" he shouted at the top of his voice, remembering the password which had come to his aid in the tunnel. It was no good. The password wasn't going to work. In next to no time Mannheim would spot him and all would be lost. But as he looked up he saw that the helicopter was not coming down after all. It remained hovering for several minutes. Then it rose in the air and took off across the sea.

That was just the right incentive to force Davey to limp and drag himself with as much speed as he could towards Stefan's cottage. As he got nearer he saw that the hall light was on and the door had been left wide open. He could see at a glance that Stefan's navy reefer jacket, the one he always wore out of doors, was missing from the pegs on the wall.

"Stefan," he yelled while knowing it was too late. He must have been shaken awake by the explosion and, hearing the alarm, gone over to the plant to save his precious project.

Ignoring the pain in his leg Davey stumbled wildly, trying to hop on his good leg between steps but his legs refused to obey him. It was like wading in treacle. He knew he'd helped to destroy the dream of the man who'd sheltered him and now he'd killed him. No one could have survived that explosion. He pushed through the debris in the dining area, through the still intact inner room and found the door to the tunnel hanging off its hinges. Smoke was pouring through from the other side and a man in a smutty white overall, coughing and choking, almost fell over him as he struggled into the room.

"Gruss Gott," said the man hoarsely.

"Stefan, have you seen Stefan?" gasped Davey.

"What I have seen?"

"Stefan Cusack...please, have you seen him?"

"Cusack...Oh...ja, he's mad. All the gates are wide open... no security. He's gone to the third gate. No chance... he...too late, everything finished... caput."

Davey hurled himself into the tunnel and the seething smoke.

"Stop, you'll be killed..." But Davey was out of hearing, his eyes bleared with smoke. The strange red lights were now extinguished and as he plunged into the darkness he could hear a distant rumbling like a second explosion about to erupt, but he had no other thought except that he must find Stefan. He stumbled on just able to make out ghostly jagged shapes, portions of shattered walls, past the first gate, past the second and into the control room where the monitors and machines were ablaze. Ahead the barred metal third gate, the place Mary had warned him about, swung on its hinges bang, banging like artillery fire. And there, hair plastered to his forehead, face blackened with smoke stood Stefan, calmly fiddling with a control panel, careless of the shooting flames and sounds that seemed to be coming from an inferno.

"Stefan, get out! Get out now!" shouted Davey, but the banging of the gate drowned his words.

Davey spurted forward and grabbed Stefan's jacket.

He turned, seeming unable to recognise the dust and dirt encrusted figure before him.

"The plant's going up, any moment," yelled Davey.

But Stefan simply gazed at him with a mournful look.

"Didn't you hear the first explosion?" Davey shouted still tugging at him.

"Yes. Got down here straight away…I got the power going again…I got it going again." Stefan shook off Davey's grip.

"Do you hear?" he yelled back, coughing and spitting out foul air and smoke. "But it's failed again"

"It's too late, you'll be killed and it'll be all my fault. Please Stefan, everyone's gone. Mannheim radioed for a helicopter but it took off again. And Uncle Eli's with him."

"Eli? Eh? Well they'll only be thinking of saving their own skins," said Stefan breathing hard. "Don't know what you're doing here but I can't do a damn thing to stop the next explosion coming and while I don't care about myself I'm not letting you go up with the works. I reckon we've less than five minutes to get clear. Come on then, there's an emergency exit if it's not blocked."

The walls around them began to vibrate and the ground shook violently as a gaping chasm opened at their feet. Pulling Davey to safety just in time Stefan guided him through the thick pall of smoke and blazing control room to a door which had been blasted off its hinges and into the tunnel which led to the emergency exit.

At last they were out in the debris strewn forecourt, gasping for breath, and for the first time Stefan registered that Davey was hurt.

"How bad is it lad? I guess we've little time now before the whole island explodes. The power boat's our only chance, it'll be a scramble to get to it, if it's not already been taken. Can you make it?

"Yes," Davey grimaced. "Just try and stop me."

They began scrambling over rocks on the far side of the settlement. "Are you all right! Need a hand?" he called back to Davey who was doing his best to keep up. "Not far, keep going."

Soon they were coming down into an inlet Davey had not seen before. It was getting light now and he could see that the powerboat was loaded with men who must have escaped at the first sign of danger.

"Quick David, they're pulling out!" Stefan began rushing towards the shore yelling to them to stop, but it was too late. As Davey came up panting and still limping the boat shot out to sea. Then they heard the sound of the whirring of a helicopter. The noise increased as the helicopter circled but it didn't land and soon took off again just as they heard another almighty explosion.

Davey looked at Stefan, a horrific thought beginning to take shape in his mind. Where was his uncle? And then he cast his eyes down as he read the answer on Stefan's face. But all Stefan said was, "That'll be the underground lab. Pity the poor beggars who didn't get out in time." Then, noticing Davey's leg which was bleeding profusely, he stripped off his outer clothes down to his shirt which he tore off and, ripping off the sleeve, wound it tightly round Davey's leg. "Now we've just one chance, the dinghy. Can you make it?" he said giving Davey a hand as they crossed the sandy shore towards the old jetty.

To their horror, as they came up to the jetty, they saw that the dinghy had come loose and was floating out to sea being tossed by the waves.

"We'll have to swim for it," said Davey.

"Can't swim," said Stefan. "It's no good David. The whole island'll soon go up in flames." The sky seemed ablaze with an intense vivid radiation.

"I'm going in after the dinghy," Davey began pulling off his torn anorak and trousers.

"Don't be stupid. The water's so cold you'll freeze to death before you reach it and with that leg............."

But Davey was already plunging from the jetty. The first impact of the freezing water seemed to paralyse his brain. He couldn't move. He seemed to have become numb all over. He tried to flail his arms and legs. He had to overcome the terrible sensation of numbness. A huge wave hit him, choking the breath out of him. He choked again, trying to take in air. Suddenly he could move.

"Acholiwai," the word came almost unbidden into his struggling mind and there, only a few feet away, the dinghy was bobbing up and down ahead of him. He was going to reach it. He went under once again.

When he surfaced he saw three grey snouts nudging the dinghy towards him. One of the dolphins swam to his side pushing him, urging him. He was filled with an unusual surge of energy as strength returned to his arms and legs. With one tremendous push the dolphin brought him close enough to the little craft for him to catch hold of the dinghy's trailing rope. Pulling until he thought his lungs would burst, he swam back with it to the jetty.

Stefan reached down, caught hold of the rope, and tied it to the iron hoop on the wall. As Davey clambered in Stefan threw Davey's clothes down.

"Strangest thing I ever saw," said Stefan lowering himself into the craft. "You'd think they knew you needed help." And they both watched as the three dolphins leapt up, their dark fins scattering showers of water, then they plunged down and soared up again, executing a triumphant dance as they became smaller and smaller on the horizon.

"Get the wet things off immediately," Stefan ordered.

Taking off his own thick pullover he rubbed Davey vigorously with it while Davey tried to pull on his trousers and finally his anorak.

"Keep the pullover on," Stefan's voice was calm and controlled.

"I may not be able to swim but I know how to master this thing," he said, pulling at the starter cord. Thankfully the boat responded immediately.

"Now all we have to hope is that neither of us dies of hypothermia before we reach land."

There was an enormous thundering sound from the island as they sped off in the dust filled air. Thick black clouds of smoke belched out as though trying to reach them and draw them back. A strong wind was picking up, whipping the sea into angry troughs. The little boat was rocking dangerously but still moving fast. As the air cleared they could see the whole horizon was crimson. Davey stirred and leaning over the side retched into the water.

Stefan stretched out a hand towards him.

"I'm all right," he muttered wiping his face on his sleeve. "I just can't help thinking about what's happened on the island."

"Too late now," said Stefan with an oddly strained and anguished look. "I just need to get you safely to land. You look all in."

Davey tried to smile. At least he was alive and so was Stefan, but he could feel himself drifting into a drowsy half sleep in which he could still sense the biting cold and twisting pain in his leg. He was drifting, dreaming. He felt sure he saw his mother's face. She was whispering to him, something about needing to stay alert. He opened his eyes. There was a thud and shuddering jar. He felt a rush of waves and white spume and a chaos of dark grey sea tearing over him.

The bow of a ship loomed above and everything went black.

Chapter 19

Davey never knew how he came to be aboard a police launch. The first thing he was aware of was being shaken by the jerking of the stretcher on which he was lying that was being heaved ashore.

He saw uniformed men, one of whom winked at him as he opened his eyes.

"You'll be fine now lad," he said. "We'll just get you and your dad to a hospital for a check over. Your dad's going to be OK. Have no fear."

Davey was bewildered and dazed. Was he dreaming? His Dad? Then he breathed a sigh of relief. He must mean Stefan. He closed his eyes from sheer weariness as the men gently placed the stretcher in a waiting ambulance.

He woke to find a nurse bending over him with a thermometer in her hand.

"Well, you'll live," she said cheerfully. "Lucky for you the launch was on the spot when your dinghy hit the rocks. I suppose you'll want to see your Dad?"

Davey was on the point of telling her that Stefan was not his dad, but somehow the idea gave him such a warm feeling he said only, "How is he?

"He's had concussion. We'll need to monitor him for a while longer."

The nurse helped Davey into a dressing gown and took him into the side ward where Stefan lay, his head swathed in bandages. He was very still and his face looked old and white.

Davey swallowed hard. 'Don't die! Please don't die!' he pleaded silently. He fought back the tears feeling hopeless and helpless. This was all his fault.

As Davey approached the bed Stefan's eyelids fluttered open and he smiled weakly.

"We made it Davey." His voice sounded thin and distant. "You were a real hero. Pity about those rocks though. We hit a beauty, didn't we?" He struggled to sit up and sank back, his eyes dark with pain.

"Don't try to talk now," said the nurse. "Davey can come to see you again shortly. He just needed to know his Dad was all right." As she turned to usher Davey out she didn't see the conspiratorial grin that passed between Davey and Stefan, weak though he was.

"You've no idea how lucky you two were," she whispered as she returned Davey to his own ward. "A boat, quite a sizeable one, capsized a few miles off the coast this morning after hitting rocks. These are dangerous waters for people who don't know them well. We're not yet sure, but it is feared there are no survivors."

Davey knew beyond doubt that it was the powerboat. He shuddered to think of his own part in the night's terrible events. Now there was probably only Stefan alive who knew the formula for the new fuel. He found himself praying that nothing would happen to Stefan. He felt more frightened and alone than he had ever felt.

If Stefan died he'd have no one at all, not even Uncle Eli in his cold bleak castle.

He heard a bleep and the nurse picked up her phone. She listened, and looking at Davey said, "You've got visitors."

His heart missed a beat. Could it be Mary or Lotharion? Who could know he was here? He nearly jumped for joy when Tom and Rob rushed in, closely followed by Mr Hughes, his headmaster.

"Well, David," Mr Hughes was saying, "we gather you've had quite an adventure. We saw the news flash this morning about a disastrous blaze on a small island north of the Western Isles and that some people trying to escape had been drowned. We did not connect it with you."

"No," broke in Uncle Tom. "It was Mary McEwen who told us and helped us to locate you. Mr Hughes drove us over post haste."

"You're to come back with us to stay in Lochlan as soon as you are ready to travel," said Rob, looking at Davey with awe and undisguised admiration.

"He could be ready whenever he chooses," said the nurse, who was bustling about the room all ears.

"But I can't go without Stefan," Davey blurted out.

"Stefan?" Mr Hughes raised his eyebrows.

"The relative I was staying with. He's in hospital too. He's hurt."

"And how long will Stefan have to stay?" Mr Hughes turned to the nurse who was now looking very puzzled.

"You know," broke in Davey, looking at the nurse, "You thought he was my Dad."

"Ah, yes," she said. "He's had a severe blow to the head. It could be a day or days. It's hard to tell in such cases, and then he'll have to wait for police enquiries."

"Police enquiries?" This was something Davey hadn't bargained for.

"Just the usual procedure. Of course they might need to interview Davey too but I shouldn't think so."

"In that case," said Mr Hughes, "if Davey can't go without Stefan there must be a hotel or lodgings where we can stay."

"There's a nice little hotel down by the harbour. Won't be much trade this time of year."

"That's it then." Mr. Hughes clapped Tom on the shoulder and grinning at Rob said, "How about a little off shore fishing? Although I suspect Davey would prefer to stay on dry land."

"Do come Pol," Rob pleaded

Davey hated saying no. He was always going off somewhere or doing something else. He wondered why Rob even bothered to stay friends.

Avoiding his friend's eyes he looked at the Head. "If it's all right sir, I'd rather stay here with Stefan until I know that he's better."

"By the way, Mary sends her regards." Tom was quick to change the subject sensing Davey's embarrassment. "She said you were not to worry about the stones, that they would be sure to turn up somewhere."

The amulets! Davey had completely forgotten about them. He began rummaging in his bedside locker. "Nurse," he called, "was I wearing an anorak when I was brought in here?"

The nurse came over and pulled out trousers and a shirt. "I think these are all you were wearing when they found you," she said. "One of the policemen who brought you in said there were no signs of identification on you except a kind of locket you were wearing."

Davey quickly felt around his neck under the collar of his dressing gown and, to his relief, his fingers closed over the Acholiwai amulet.

His mother's protective amulet was still there, but the others were lost and yet Mary knew about that already.

"I've something to tell you. When you're better." Seeing Davey's face pale Tom quickly added, "It's good news Davey, very good news."

"Best we don't heap everything on the boy at once," said Mr Hughes. "Come on Rob. You two will have plenty of time to chat later."

"You bet! Loads," said Rob, reluctantly following the grown-ups as they let the ward. "See you tomorrow then, Pol," he called.

* * *

Stefan was sitting up when Davey saw him next day. His eyes looked brighter and there was a little more colour in his face. He pressed Davey's hand and Davey felt a rush of relief. Stefan was going to be fine.

"The nurse said there might be police enquiries," he blurted out, immediately regretting his clumsiness." What do you think they'll want to know?"

"Routine things I guess," said Stefan not wanting to worry the boy.

"Will they be able to connect us with what happened on Torksay?" Davey shifted uneasily.

"What? After that massive bonfire?" Stefan's tone indicating he had no doubts.

"And," Davey stammered "Uncle Eli?"

"Pretty conclusive, I would say," he said softly.

"But they're bound to want to know what we were doing in that area at that time so soon after the explosions, and," Davey hesitated, "you're the only one left to take the blame. The powerboat sank yesterday. There were no survivors."

Stefan shivered visibly. "They were fine scientists. It is very sad and a great loss. I must have been a fool not to see where those experiments could lead. It was a lunatic venture." They both remained silent for some time.

"But David, who's to associate either of us with the Torksay disaster? You're my nephew, if we stretch the imagination," he smiled. "We were out on an early morning fishing trip, you fell overboard and then we crashed into rocks. I have my passport and an address registered at Leith. Do your friends know anything to the contrary?"

"They knew I was staying with you for a few days....nothing more. So there's no-one who knows about it, about the fuel and the Mannheim project?"

"Only me, but I think I can safely say I have conveniently forgotten the formula and the process," said Stefan wryly, then grimacing as he felt the pain shoot through his head.

"So it's really finished, and no-one's going to try to start anything like that again?" Davey couldn't keep the triumph out of his voice.

"I wouldn't be too sure. There'll always be someone, maybe like me, blind to everything except the fascination of getting the experiment to succeed, not counting the cost." Stefan sighed deeply. Davey knew he must have been thinking about the terrible power of a minute drop of a fuel that could cause such massive destruction.

"Someone, somewhere will try again Davey. People soon forget. They don't learn easily. Look at me, blinded by my own pride. And Eli and Mannheim, both fanatics too in their way."

"What will you do now?"

"As soon as I'm out of here there'll be no more experiments like that I assure you. Do you know? I might even come to your school and teach. If they'll have me," he added playfully.

He grinned at Davey who suddenly felt happier than he had felt for a long time, until a sobering thought struck him.

"If only," he said forlornly. "But there's still Olga and.......I'll have to go back to Kilkune"

"Why? Do you really want to?"

"No! I don't ever want to go back there again," Davey said with passion. "Except perhaps to see Billy and his mother."

"Perhaps there are things, your own things, you'll need to go back to collect?"

"No, there's nothing," then he remembered. "Well one thing, perhaps two. You may think it odd but Uncle Eli kept my chest of drawers and my wooden bed. They were special, with Polish dancers painted on them. They were all I had left.....after my parents........" he stammered. "I would like them back."

"That's no problem. But are you sure they're yours?"

"Dead sure. Why?"

"That's odd. I remember your cousin Boris having exactly the same set. Eli never let anyone else touch them after Boris died. Perhaps it was sentimentality that made him keep yours."

Before Davey had time to digest this the nurse came in to say Davey's friends had arrived and the police would like to talk to Mr Cusack, if he was feeling up to it.

"Everything'll work out." Stefan squeezed Davey's shoulder as he left with the nurse.

When Rob came in with the grown ups he began to launch into an account of the morning's fishing trip but Tom, speaking quietly, interrupted him saying he had something to say that couldn't wait.

"Mary gave me some information that affects you greatly Davey. It is about the inheritance left by your grandfather. Since you are the only son of the eldest Jampolski, you will be entitled to it when you reach eighteen."

Davey listened attentively as he continued. "The money, in the event of anything happening to your parents before you reached that age, was to be managed by a relative or guardian. As you know, it is believed your uncle perished in the island fire, at least according to Mary McEwen."

So it was true. Mary would know. Davey held his breath and said nothing.

"There were serious charges against your uncle and his wife, Olga, concerning tax evasion and illegal dumping of toxic waste. When Olga recovers she will be liable, as the remaining partner, to face heavy fines and possibly a prison sentence."

"Mary has known all this for some time," said Davey breathing more freely now.

"Yes, she said so, but she was quite adamant that she was unable to reveal the facts until now. She didn't explain, but I believe she had good reason."

And Davey knew exactly what those reasons were. Had Eli been rumbled too early Mannheim and the whole project would have been alerted. With advance warning they could have closed down operations and moved them elsewhere without being detected.

"Poor old Uncle Eli," said Davey at last. "I know what harm he has caused, but he couldn't have been all bad."

"You might be right. I think he was to be pitied, especially as he always thought of Boris as his own son. That must have been a bitter blow."

Davey looked at Tom in utter puzzlement. "What do you mean? Boris was his son. Mary told me how very fond he was of him."

"Ironically no, he was not." Tom paused. "This may come as a shock to you but Boris was Olga's son by Karl, your father."

Davey stared at Tom, as though he had struck him. Stefan had helped him to feel close to his father again by talking about Poland and his family. And now at a stroke it was being taken away again.

"Mary said Olga told Eli the truth about Boris when they were in hospital, believing herself to be on her deathbed. I suppose Olga felt that had Boris lived he would have been entitled to the family inheritance."

Tom's firm, sympathetic hand on his shoulder told him it was the truth.

"Is that why she hated me so much?"

"I can't answer that. I just know I found it beyond belief when Mary told me how Olga had planned to harm you. No doubt she'll have plenty of time in prison to consider that."

Mr Hughes looked distinctly uncomfortable but Rob gave Davey a reassuring glance.

"Your grandfather's will, as I said, indicates the need for a relative or guardian to manage your affairs until you reach the age of eighteen. Mary suggested it could be the family lawyer."

Davey was on the point of disagreeing when Tom continued with, "By the way, Mary sends her love, says she'll write to you. She's been called away urgently to do a job in Brazil."

Davey smiled a secret smile to himself. So that's why she and Lotharion hadn't come to see him.

"She also wanted you to know that since the lease on the castle and estate would shortly run out, the Laird would be taking it on himself. He has plans, she said, to turn the castle into a study centre and the estate into a nature reserve. Both Billy and Mrs McGraw will be found work there."

"That's great news, although I shall miss Mary. And, Uncle Tom," he said, eyes suddenly gleaming with excitement, "I do have a relative of sorts."

Tom looked at him curiously, "Meaning?"

"Meaning. . .Stefan," Davey blurted out. "He wants to give up scientific experiments and become a teacher, or," suddenly having a brilliant idea, "run a study centre."

For such a long time everything had been against him. He couldn't remember when he'd felt so awake, so alive, so joyful. "He'd make a super guardian."

"We'll have to see what Stefan says first. Stefan eh?" was all Tom said. But looking at Davey's dancing eyes he knew Davey was going to win this time.